WITH

FLIRT...

BY
SAMANTHA HUNTER

® MILLS & BOON®
Pure reading pleasure

All the characters in this book have no existence outside the imagination of the author, and have no relation whatsoever to anyone bearing the same name or names. They are not even distantly inspired by any individual known or unknown to the author, and all the incidents are pure invention.

First published in Great Britain 2007
by Harlequin Mills & Boon Limited,
Eton House, 18-24 Paradise Road, Richmond, Surrey TW9 1SR

© Samantha Hunter 2006

ISBN: 978 0 263 85598 2

14-1107

Harlequin Mills & Boon policy is to use papers that are natural, renewable and recyclable products and made from wood grown in sustainable forests. The logging and manufacturing processes conform to the legal environmental regulations of the country of origin.

Printed and bound in Spain
by Litografia Rosés S.A., Barcelona

1

EJ SLOWLY LIFTED from his sex-induced slumber, feeling a soft hand curl around his morning erection, stroking him into further wakefulness. He groaned and stretched, not opening his eyes, but moving into the hand that held him, fueling the caress. Finally, he spoke, his voice hoarse and good-humored.

"I'm dead, Jo. You did me in last night."

"You don't feel dead to me."

There was an unmistakable smile in her voice, and a clear promise of more sensual adventures. But he really was exhausted.

He'd met Jo a little less than twenty-four hours ago; she'd been the instructor for his sky-jumping lesson the day before. He'd never parachuted before, but he'd decided to do something special for his thirty-fifth birthday. So first he'd jumped out of the plane. Then, exhilarated by the adrenaline rush and ready to go out and celebrate, he'd ended up jumping Jo, as well. Or maybe she'd jumped him. The end result was the same.

He'd had to put the family celebration off until the

weekend, which hadn't pleased his mother one bit. But all in all, it had been a good birthday, he thought with a grin, feeling the pleasure of Jo's practiced touch course through him.

"That feels wonderful, darlin', but I have to get to work."

"Won't take long, *darlin'*," Jo laughed. She loved making fun of his Southern accent, and he didn't mind one bit. He was the product of four generations of Virginian tradition and she was pure Connecticut Yankee. But when a woman was as warm and passionate in bed as Jo was, he could care less about geographical differences.

EJ loved all kinds of women. As evidence of the fact, he'd dated as many as time and opportunity allowed in the past few years, since he'd ended his romance with his childhood friend, Millie Stewart. EJ had broken their engagement, left his job with the family shipbuilding business, and basically thrown the seriousness and responsibility of his old life to the wind. He loved his freedom, he loved his job and he loved women. Life was good.

EJ sometimes wondered what had driven him to want to get married and have kids in the first place. Well, he knew the answer to that: family pressure. Being Ethan Jared Beaumont the Fourth came with a set of expectations, especially after his father had died unexpectedly of a heart attack five years ago.

EJ had quit his job with the Department of Justice,

where he'd worked as a fraud investigator, and filled the seat left empty by his dad—Ethan Jared Beaumont the Third. EJ had done his duty. And he'd been miserable. He just hadn't known it. Then his friend Ian Chandler had offered him the job of a lifetime with a specialized computer crime unit, known as the "HotWires" team. They worked in conjunction with the Norfolk Police Department, and EJ had never regretted for one moment accepting Ian's offer.

That was almost three years ago. And now, his life was better than he ever could have imagined.

"Maybe I can breathe a little life into you?" Jo smiled, her tone hushed and suggestive as she slid down his body under the covers intending to replace her hand with her mouth, but he reached out, stopping her.

"I'm sorry, honey, I really do have to get to work. I have a meeting in less than an hour."

Jo settled back, sighing. "Well, okay then. I suppose I should get going, too." She smiled in a friendly way, as if they were simply having a casual chat on the sidewalk instead of crawling out of bed after hours of vigorous sex. "I had a great time, thanks."

She slid off the bed and walked around the room in totally unselfconscious nudity, picking up her clothes. EJ sat up, too, wondering why he was suddenly disgruntled and out of sorts. He was tired, and he'd passed up an award-winning blow job, for sure, but Jo didn't seem to be all that concerned about his refusal. There was no problem with rejection, no pouting, no argument.

She walked over to him, smiling, and kissed him goodbye. A friendly peck. For some reason, it pissed him off.

"Can I pop in your shower for a minute?" She looked him in the eye, no trace of any hidden agenda. Not an iota of disappointment. He shook his head, erasing his errant thoughts, and hauled her up against him. Bending to kiss her soft breast, he pushed aside whatever was bothering him.

"Sure. Maybe I'll join you for a quick one."

CHARLEY: You're very expressive. You enjoy it when someone tells you what they want in bed, where to touch them, how to kiss you....

EJB: I do like that—how did you know?

CHARLEY: Your cards show your strong need for communication and sensuality in a relationship. You need to be with someone who can excite your mind as well as your body—with what they say, how they eat or cook, the music they appreciate.

EJB: Would you tell me where to touch you? How to kiss you?

CHARLEY: I'm a very verbal person, yes.

EJB: I get turned on by a woman telling me

what she wants to do, and what she wants me to
do to her.

CHARLEY: I know....

"Sheesh, EJ—pouring it on a little thick,
weren't you?"

EJ slid his glasses off and rubbed his eyes, tired
from being up too late and getting in just under the
wire to pour over the transcripts of his last dialogue
with the suspect he was currently investigating. Not
that his quickie in the shower with Jo hadn't been
worth it, but he wasn't in the habit of being late to work
because of sex. Work was first on his list, and he took
it seriously.

Sarah Jessup, one of his partners on the team, was
skimming over the transcript as well, looking at him
in mock disgust.

"I mean, really. Do women fall for this *schlock?*"
He grinned, loving the Yiddish words Sarah
always threw into the conversation that he'd never
be able to pull off with his southern drawl. But Sarah
was born and raised near New York City, and she'd
spent almost a decade in Brooklyn before moving
to Norfolk, Virginia, to be one of the team, so she
could definitely talk the talk. Her three years living
below the Mason-Dixon Line hadn't changed her
hard-edged New York attitude one bit. EJ loved it.

"They fall right into bed, darlin'. All except for
you, of course."

"Yeah, I'm immune to your flirting, thank God."

"I didn't really try all that hard, us working together and all."

"Yuh-huh. You keep telling yourself that."

"Ah, now. No need to be bitter. All this reading here is all playacting. Couldn't blame you one bit if it makes you wonder what you missed out on."

He grinned, watching her gorgeous blue eyes narrow—there was nothing romantic between them and never had been, but he loved teasing her about her "missed opportunity." He'd made a pass at Sarah once, years ago, before she'd met the man she was currently engaged to, Logan Sullivan. Logan was a former cop who was currently starting his own kayak sales and service business.

EJ knew he'd been out of line propositioning Sarah in the first place, but they'd been alone, out having a few drinks after finishing a case, and they were both single and lonely. At the time, he'd just broken his engagement and wasn't sure what was in store for him. And Sarah had been available, and he liked her. He'd figured, why not?

Sarah had put EJ in his place. She wasn't interested in falling into bed with anyone, period, but especially not with someone at the office. Of course, six months ago Logan had come along and changed all that, seducing Sarah when they met on a vacation fling, and then becoming her ad hoc partner while solving a missing person case that had cracked open one of the largest Internet pornography operations on the east coast. Sarah was all work, all the time, even when she'd been on vacation. Logan had mellowed her a bit, but not much.

The bust had been a huge feather in Sarah's cap professionally, but meeting Logan and putting some of her own ghosts to rest while doing so had made Sarah a happier person, in general. She was still intense, but she just was more peaceful overall, more settled. Well, settled might be overstating it.

EJ was always grateful that she hadn't taken him up on his offer that night, though he sure enjoyed teasing her about it. They had a solid friendship and a perfect working relationship, and that was all. That was enough. In many ways, he was closer to Sarah than he was with any of the women he slept with.

Sarah quirked an eyebrow. "You're looking a little tired this morning, EJ. Worn out. Was last night's birthday conquest a little too athletic for you, old man?" She grinned. "Many happy returns, but the way."

He winced, hating that she'd hit on the source of his tiredness spot-on, but aimed a no-nonsense look in her direction instead. "Thanks. When do you leave again?"

Sarah didn't miss his sarcasm, but broke into a huge grin. The change in topic was obviously a happy one for her.

"Two weeks."

"Damn. I thought it was sooner."

EJ watched her shape her fingers into a gun and

shoot him point-blank. He loved messing with Sarah, and he loved it that she gave as good as she got. She was a breath of fresh air, a whole different species than the well-heeled, upper-class Southern women he'd grown up with.

He glanced at his e-mail, skimming the subject lines of incoming mail that already had piled up in his inbox, realizing the room had become very quiet. He looked over and smiled more sincerely, finding her lost in thought as she gazed at the huge diamond on her left hand.

"It's a helluva rock. Logan really wants you to have the best."

She blushed furiously and then glared at him—if Sarah hated anything, it was being caught acting girly. She was tough as nails, a great cop, and a brilliant computer hacker. But Logan had also brought out her softer side in a big way. The glare morphed into a cheeky smile as she flitted her fingers in the air.

"It *is* amazing, but it's just a ring. Having Logan is what counts. And in two weeks, I will be on an amazing honeymoon with an amazing man having amazing sex all day on our own amazing private beach."

EJ sighed exaggeratedly. "Another one gone to the other side."

"Yeah, just wait. Your turn is coming."

"Thanks, but no thanks. I'm happy just the way I am."

She just gave him a look of doubt—or maybe it was something else. Concern? It was often annoying now that he'd discovered the wilder side of life, that all of his friends were settling down with spouses and babies. And the more that happened, the more they believed it should happen to him, too.

Maybe someday he would find someone special. Fill his empty family home and grow old with grandchildren on his knee. There would be a time when the singles life wouldn't appeal quite as much, and he didn't want to get old alone. But that time wasn't now.

Shaking his head, he silently thanked the heavens when their boss—and his old friend—Ian Chandler walked into the office, putting an end to the discussion and turning matters to business. Ian was a few minutes late, and looking even more exhausted than EJ, but that was bound to happen when his wife was expecting twins at any moment.

Ian had met his wife, Sage, at the same time the HotWires team had been forming. It had been a bumpy courtship to say the least, but all was well that ended well. EJ thought the world of them both, and was happy to be included in their little family by being asked to be future godfather to the babies. For EJ, it was the best of all possible worlds—he got to enjoy things like babies and friends, weddings and family, but he also had his independence.

"Morning, folks."

"Hey, Daddy. How're my goddaughters?"

EJ watched pride replace the exhaustion as Ian sat down to start their meeting.

"Ready to come out and driving their mama crazy already, kicking and keeping her up at night. Sage is big as a house, and still trying to work, even though the doctor has her on partial bed rest. I have no idea what to do to make that woman slow down."

EJ laughed. "Neither one of you will be slowing down for a while, I suspect. But at least you got her to marry you."

"Yeah."

EJ watched his friend's eyes warm as he glanced at the gold band on his finger that had been placed there four months before. Busy with their lives and with Sage starting a new business, Ian and Sage had ended up pregnant before they'd talked about marriage. Both of them had been happy enough with the new development. Though Sage had been hesitant to have a shotgun wedding, in the end Ian had won her over and it had been a beautiful event, made even richer by the knowledge that they would soon be a family.

The sentimental look vanished as Ian turned to business.

"So you've made contact?"

EJ nodded. "Last night was our second meeting."

"Anything notable?"

"Here's the transcript." He ignored Sarah's

chuckle as he shoved a file folder in Ian's direction. "But no, not much. Yet. It's early."

"It may take a little while. They could be feeling you out."

EJ agreed, but he was still hoping to crack this case sooner than later. If nothing else, he was getting tired of online sex talk—he liked his sex real and in person.

They'd been working on the paper trail for weeks, tracing scattered evidence regarding large thefts that had no seeming connection, but after sifting through piles of notes and paperwork, one commonality finally appeared: all of the victims had been subscribers to an online psychic service called SexyTarot.com.

Finally, EJ was closing in. That single, real thread of evidence had led them right to their own backyard: Norfolk, Virginia. Said service was owned by a single player: Charlotte Gerard. That was the common denominator among all the people who had lost money—at one time or another, she'd read for the victims.

He focused back on the file. A background check had revealed zip in the way of a criminal past, though Ms. Gerard had experienced a less than stellar childhood. Raised an orphan up north in New Hampshire, she went the usual route and lived in several foster homes until she'd moved to Norfolk three years ago. She didn't own a car and had no priors, but that didn't mean she wasn't a late bloomer to a life of crime.

Ms. Gerard was twenty-nine, single, and eighteen months ago she'd started running SexyTarot.com, which offered psychic readings focusing specifically on clients' love lives.

It seemed innocent enough on the surface, but the service was an ideal cover for luring people in and gaining information that could lead to bank accounts, credit cards and even home addresses. However, the catch was that other than the circumstantial evidence of all victims having paid for readings, EJ couldn't find any hard evidence connecting the woman directly to the thefts—yet. It was his job to get it.

Ian looked at him speculatively. "What's your gut telling you?"

"That the sooner I can drag her out from behind the screen, the sooner I can get this settled. I'm hoping I can force her hand if I set myself up as a target she can't resist. A chance for one big score."

"What are you thinking about?"

He grinned, winking at Sarah and watching her roll her eyes. "Just a little not-so-innocent flirtation. I figure heating things up a little and trying to draw her out, maybe for a date, would be the easiest way to go. It happens online all the time these days and is unlikely to cause any suspicion. At worst, she'll think I'm an online pervert and say no. But if she's checked me out via the registration information and card info I gave her, I think she'll bite."

"Then do it. You're certain the woman you're interacting with is Charlotte Gerard?"

EJ smiled, but there was a slight predatory gleam in his eye—he loved tracking down the bad guy, or bad girl, as the case had it.

"Sure as I can be. Goes by 'Charley'—not exactly a masterful disguise. But meeting her for real will cement things, if I can get her to go for it."

"Good. Remember, she could just be a little fish fronting a larger scam, which is why we can't find anything tied directly to her—could be she just lures in the marks, and the real action goes down somewhere else."

EJ nodded, still looking at the photo, wondering what pushed a young woman like Charlotte into a career of crime. She looked like a sweet thing, paid her taxes even on the pittance she appeared to earn on the Web site and at odd jobs. She was, perhaps, a little too squeaky clean. Unfortunately, EJ knew he lived in a world where if someone was too clean, they were probably dirty.

She'd been engaging, entertaining and yet apparently sincere while she'd read for him the night before. And sexy, without a doubt. She'd said things to him that scored a direct hit on his desires—he loved a woman who wasn't afraid to talk about sex in frank terms. A female voice saying the right thing in his ear could turn him on faster than any touch.

Charlotte was particularly talented at drawing him

into the conversation, making him lose track of his objective and almost luring him into admitting some things that he didn't easily discuss with anyone. What he wanted in bed and from life. From love.

He dismissed it as the same phenomenon as airplane talk. Talking with people online was a lot like talking to strangers in airplanes—you could say anything, because you were never going to see them again.

But deep down, he also knew there was a grain of truth to the things he'd shared with Charlotte, and he didn't like how she'd pulled him in to whatever spell she wove. In general, he considered himself immune to that kind of thing, and it rankled that he'd felt a sense of connection when he should have been concentrating only on business. She was a suspect, for crying out loud.

But her smooth ability to get people to feel comfortable, to get them to talk, was even more proof against her—in his gut, anyway. The best con artists were very hard to dislike and they knew how to read people, how to get the information they needed. But so did EJ.

EJ looked back at Ian, changing the subject. "So how are you and Sage holding up?"

"I'm fine, but I feel for Sage. She's so big, and mostly immobile, which is torture for her. She's so used to being on the go, and was at a really critical point with her consulting business when she found out about the babies. She's conducting business online and over the phone, but she's tired and more than a little cranky."

Sarah butted in, shuddering. "Who could blame her? I get cranky just thinking about it."

"You're cranky anyway," Ian teased. "Aren't you and Logan thinking about a family?"

"Sure. In about ten or fifteen years. Or longer."

EJ tipped his head curiously. "Have you ever heard of the concept of a biological clock?"

Sarah grinned smugly. "They make them digital these days. Women are having babies in their forties and beyond. Although I don't really get that, either."

EJ and Ian shook their heads, laughing. Sarah was incorrigible. Logan had often talked about a family, especially inspired by Sage and Ian, but Sarah was holding strong. Having babies was not in the cards for her anytime soon, EJ imagined. Logan would have his work cut out for him.

Conversation ceased as Ian grabbed his cell phone, excusing himself for a moment. Looking past the clear glass windows that encased their offices, the hallways of the Norfolk Police Department buzzed with activity. Outside the office, he knew it would be hot and muggy—the air-conditioning was constantly on the blitz, but the HotWires offices were almost too cold, kept that way because of the sensitive technology in the room.

They'd come a long way in three years, solving some major cases, and increasing their funding and resources with each success. It had just been the three of them to start, an experiment that had met with phenomenal success. Their unit, having gained state and local recognition for their work, had just gotten more funds to expand. The cases were piling up, and they needed more people on the job, especially with their personal lives becoming more complicated.

In fact, Ian was lining up interviews with prospective agents soon. EJ looked over at Sarah, who returned to her case file with deep concentration. She'd been a freelance computer hacker just a few years ago, doing odd jobs so she could finance her hacking habit, buying all the computer equipment she needed to track down Internet pornographers so she could report them to the feds. It was how she'd met Ian and had ended up being a part of the team. And she was one damned good cop; Ian had great instincts, and hiring Sarah had paid off big-time.

But EJ had thought further ahead. In fact, should Ian ever decide to change jobs, considering his family situation, EJ hoped to be able to step up to the plate to lead the HotWires unit, something his single life prepared him for perfectly.

He'd never spoken to Ian about it, but he wondered if his friend would want to stay in a dangerous position after he had children to consider. Having stared down the barrel of a gun more than once in the line of duty, EJ wasn't sure he could do it if he had little ones depending on him to come home every night.

Ian's voice brought EJ back to the moment. "I'll be spending more time at home, but I'm still available if you need me in here. And Sarah can be pulled in, too, if you need backup. At least before she leaves. If you can't get us, you're authorized through Marty to pull whatever you need from the general department resources."

EJ nodded, looking again at the petite blonde with the heart-shaped face in the photograph, and he felt a stirring in his gut, remembering what this beautiful woman had talked about with him online. Private, intimate, sexy things.

Too bad she was probably going to jail.

2

THE THREE OF SWORDS crossed by *The Devil* yet again—poor Ronny. Charlotte sighed, looking for something good in the cards—she always tried to put a positive spin on things, if she could—but this reading bothered her. In fact, it gave her a creepy feeling; something was definitely off in her brother's life. As usual.

Ronny never asked for readings—he thought her tarot was a bunch of hooey—but now and then she did a reading for him, just for herself, to get an idea how his life was going and how she could support or advise him. Normally she would never do a reading without someone's permission—it was eavesdropping of a kind—but this was her privilege as a big sister, she figured.

Padding into the small kitchen of her apartment on Ocean View, just east of downtown Norfolk, she poured herself a large glass of lemongrass iced tea and stared out the small window over her old-fashioned ceramic kitchen sink as she sipped.

Her apartment wasn't in the fanciest of buildings,

in fact, it was probably going to be knocked down sooner than later to make way for the new development that was springing up left and right. But she stayed here because she was in love with the view.

Four miles of quiet beach stretched out on either side of her backyard. The southern end of the Chesapeake Bay was only about eighty-two steps outside her back door—she'd counted—and she had a panoramic view of the famous Bay Bridge.

If she went out her front door, the road was busy, and the streets were not ones she was comfortable walking too late at night, though it was safer now that they'd decided to redevelop the more dangerous areas on the southernmost end of the avenue. Things were picking up; there were new businesses, homes and a golf course.

But it was the mix of people, the way new condos sprouted up between fleabag hotels and old apartment houses like hers, and how tidy, older ladies walked their prissy little poodles alongside kids with sagging pants and MP3 players that attracted her. The place had personality and diversity, and the entire neighborhood was eclectic and genuine. She felt like she fit right in.

She stared at the cards again, her thoughts returning to her brother. He'd had a hard time of it, and it didn't look like anything was going to get easier, which broke her heart. She'd only known him for three years. She'd found him through a family locator service that helped siblings separated by the courts to find each other again. It had taken her almost ten years, since she was eighteen, to find him. She'd continued the search in fits and starts as money and time allowed.

She'd lived in New Hampshire then, the land of the White Mountains and presidential primaries, but she never regretted moving to Virginia to be near Ronny. He wasn't able to move, and she didn't mind. She was more flexible, able to work wherever she went. But, in truth, she would have lived just about anywhere to be near the only family she had.

"Hey, Mary, Mary…how does your garden grow?"

Ronny's voice boomed as he walked through the front door, and she quickly slid the cards into the deck, gasping in delighted surprise when she saw he was carrying several flats of colorful flowers.

Because she worked planting and maintaining flowerboxes—one of her more profitable ventures—he always called her Mary, from the nursery rhyme. She loved it—it seemed like one of those things that a brother would do. She intercepted him before he put the flats on her clean tablecloth, and set them gently on the floor by the door.

She ran her hands over the delicate petals of colorful pansies, smiling. "These are gorgeous. Like little cheerful faces, aren't they?" She smiled up at him. "You shouldn't have, though. I know things are tight for you."

He leaned over, kissing her soundly on the cheek.

"We help each other out—that's what family does. Use these to make some boxes for out front, and make up a little sign about your flowerboxes. Maybe you'll get some new business."

Her heart swelled—she loved him so much, even though they hadn't known each other very long. True, Ronny had a rough side. He gambled, smoked pot and hung around with a rough crowd. He was on his third job in the past year, but this one seemed to be working out a little better. He had a good heart, she knew that. If only she could get him to see he was worth more than he thought he was.

"Thank you—that's a great idea. I'll do that today." She went to the counter, putting on a pot of coffee. She didn't drink it but kept it around for Ronny. He snagged the pretty towel she put on the hook that morning on his way through the kitchen, and she straightened it reflexively before reaching up to pull his cup from the spot where she kept it among her neatly arranged cupboards.

"Did you check out that brochure with the college courses I left for you?"

She heard his heavy sigh behind her. Ronny had gotten his GED, but he didn't seem interested in doing more. Charlotte hadn't been to college, either, but she liked the jobs she took to make a living. Someday, if she was able, she dreamed of opening her own flower shop, or maybe a greenhouse. But if that never happened, she enjoyed her life just as it was.

But Ronny, well, he needed focus. He needed to do something more productive with his life—just being successful at one thing might make all the difference. That's what one of his substance-abuse counselors had told her. He needed to build his self-esteem and believe he was worth success. It was her sincere wish to help him be happy, to make his life better. It wasn't always easy.

"I wish you'd drop that. I'm not college material," he grumbled.

The same old line. But she wasn't going to give up, and responded cheerfully.

"What is that supposed to mean? You're smart—look at the idea you just came up with. Ideas like that could lead to a good job."

"I have a good job. Working at the docks pays good, and in six months I get benefits."

She saw the familiar sullen look come into his eyes—they were the same soft brown as hers—as he turned away and backed off. She knew him well enough to know she couldn't push; he would just withdraw deeper into himself and become surly and unreachable.

"I'm sorry. You do, I know. And it sounds like it's going well." She looked at him from under her lashes, gently inquiring as she thought about the cards from his reading. "Things are going well, aren't they?"

"Yeah." He glanced around the kitchen, avoiding her eyes. "Um, do you mind if I check e-mail on your laptop?"

Charlotte nodded her head. "Let me boot it up for you."

"I can do it." He stood, taking the coffee she handed him. "Got any donuts?"

"You know I don't eat refined sugars."

He grinned, shaking his head. "Yeah, I don't get that."

He kissed her again, lightly on the forehead, and made his way over to the computer. She cringed a little when he picked it up and plopped it on his lap. It was her prize possession; she'd had to plant a lot of flowers and walk a lot of dogs to pay for that secondhand computer, but it was helping her expand her horizons.

Though she'd sold some things through online auctions for a small profit, her most successful venture so far was reading tarot for her online business, SexyTarot.com. While she was never going to get rich doing tarot readings, she was getting more clients as time went on, and she was helping people, as well. She truly believed that money, while necessary, wasn't always the most important thing. At first SexyTarot.com had been free, but then repeat clients had wanted to make donations, the equivalent of tipping a waitress, she supposed. Several of them were relatively generous.

She heard Ronny curse, followed by a *thunk*, and she jumped around to find him hitting the side of the computer's delicate screen.

"Ronny, please don't do that!"

"This connection's so slow. How do you ever get anything done?"

She looked at him and sighed. "Patience, I guess."

And she needed loads of it, reminding herself that the machine was just a machine, and not worth hurting her brother's feelings over. Still, she'd worked hard for everything she owned, from the kitchen towel to the laptop, and she treasured her possessions. Still, she'd trade them all rather than lose her brother.

"I think I'll go out and get started on these flowers."

"Yeah, you have a ball, doll."

She smiled, loving when he called her sweet names. It was the first time anyone in her life had ever really used endearments toward her, and it felt like a hug every time. That got her through a lot of rough moments.

She walked outside into the morning sun, thinking about what flowers she could plant first. It would definitely cheer up the dilapidated outside of the building, and be a little advertising for her, as Ronny said. She'd have to get some poster board and make up a sign later.

She opened the bag of potting dirt and sank the trowel in, losing herself in thought as she planted. Connection with natural things eased her mind and improved her mood, as always. And she'd been a little more agitated the last few days. The feeling that things in life were about to shift followed her—the sense that change was on the way. Her cards supported the theory, and she even had an inkling what it might be.

EJB.

That's the name by which she knew the man who had come to her for readings twice now, and reading for him had touched her deeply. He was a good man. He'd given her a nice donation the very first night, but that wasn't why he was special. His charisma, intelligence and responsiveness in their conversations had reached out and pulled her in. She felt like they were connected though they had never met.

Charlotte read for a lot of people, and they talked about many intimate things, but she'd never had the sense of involvement that she'd felt with EJB. She wanted to be open to it, even though it scared her a little.

She'd see him again tonight, or rather, talk to him on the chat site where she did her readings. His questions so far had been more subtle than most—the first time he'd asked her "How can I find what I'm looking for?" and the second, "Where is the woman who can give me what I want?"

Right here, handsome.

He was *The King of Cups* and *The Magician* all rolled into one. Maybe a bit of *The Devil* thrown in, as well. No doubt about it, EJB was a sensualist, and a romantic. But she felt that his sensuality was being stifled, poured into other areas of his life, but not finding its fullest expression in love.

Heat moved through her as she thought of him. She caught herself poking the tender stem and roots of a plant into the dirt a little more roughly than intended, and whispered an apology to the little blossom. She fussed, focusing on her task for a moment; counting out the number of plants she had available, she divided them evenly, to make sure she had enough of each color for the boxes.

Sitting back, she tamped the back of her cotton gardening glove to her forehead—it was going to be very warm today—and sighed. Her romantic thoughts about EJB were foolish notions, but she wished she could meet someone who had some… depth. It would be great to experience something more romantic than the propositions she regularly got from Ronny's less than desirable friends. Years in group and foster homes had taught her to be cautious when it came to men and sex. She'd never been abused, fortunately, but she'd had friends who were.

It wasn't that she was afraid of men. She'd had a few lovers—youthful relationships borne of curiosity and affection yet nothing lasting—but she was never a girl to just fall into bed with anyone who offered. She and Ronny had been the children of a woman who had been promiscuous and careless in her sexual encounters, leaving her babies at the hospital for social services to take almost as soon as they'd been born.

Charlotte would never do that—she'd gone without family for so long that she could never leave a child behind. But she didn't plan on ever having to make that decision. She wasn't a one-night stand kind of girl; she wanted something more. She wanted romance. Real, honest-to-goodness love and romance. And maybe children, someday.

She selected some tiny Coleus specimens to plant around the base of the pansies—one of her secrets was to plant boxes with several tiers that developed over time—to shade the roots and retain the moisture in the southern heat. If the little purple-and-green leaves were pruned just right, they would remain small and low, covering the dirt of the box and providing lush background color for the flowers, and protecting the dirt from hard rains that often came with afternoon storms. It was like creating a tiny forest.

Her thoughts drifted back to EJB. She wondered what his real name was, and what he looked like. And if she dared to ask him. She was trying to run a professional service, and didn't want to scare him away by being forward. He was a client who came to her for insight, after all. He'd trusted her with some of his innermost secrets and thoughts, spoken of his desires and needs. She couldn't take advantage of that, though in their last discussion, when he'd asked her if she would tell him what she wanted, how to kiss her, she'd almost given in.

A riff of anticipation made her smile to herself as

she finished one of the boxes—while she wasn't one to wish her time away, she couldn't wait to chat with him online again that evening.

EJ STRETCHED OUT on the beat-up leather sofa that dominated the den in his family home in Ghent, an upscale neighborhood close to downtown Norfolk. Though he loved the house, he didn't spend much time here. In fact, he knew that deep down he was avoiding being here more than he had to. It had just gotten too quiet. Unless he had company—especially of the female variety—he would rather be out and about, doing something interesting, rather than haunting around the huge house on his own.

His mother had moved into a smaller house that their family owned near the shore shortly after his father had passed on, and his sister, Grace, lived downtown to be close to the office. It was a big house for one man, but he couldn't part with it. He'd grown up here, a bustling place with beautiful gardens, filled with children, guests and pets. Maybe it would be again one day. His sister might get married, have children. She would probably want to live in the house, should that happen, and he would gladly find his own place.

Maybe he'd get a dog—walking dogs was supposed to be another good way to meet women. But that would probably require getting some little froufrou pooch, and he wasn't up for that. Nah, if he got a canine friend, it would be a man's dog—a Great

Dane or maybe a Lab or a Weimaraner. A solid hunting dog.

He hadn't been hunting since he was a boy. When he and his dad would drive to the Virginia woods, they'd spend more time talking than hunting. Still he'd snagged a few ducks and some deer in his younger years. A dog would come in handy for hunting. Right now though, he was gone far too much with his job to have the responsibility of a pet.

It was dark, and the crickets were singing out in the yard. Still musing, he filled his wineglass, settling back and waiting for his appointment to begin; he had a few minutes yet. But surprisingly, just as he was about to switch to another window, the Sexy-Tarot logo appeared on his screen, and Charley's sign-on signaled him that she was there. Early.

CHARLEY: Hi, EJB—are you ready? I know I'm a little early. My last appointment ended sooner than I thought.

EJB: No problems, I hope.

CHARLEY: None at all. How are you tonight?

EJB: Happy to be talking with you again. I've looked forward to this all day.

CHARLEY: Me, too.

EJ blinked—her direct response interested him. Was this the beginning of something new? His senses went on immediate alert.

EJB: Really?

CHARLEY: Yes. I was thinking about you…I mean, your cards, a lot today.

EJB: Why? Did something worry you?

CHARLEY: No, I was just moved by your last reading. There were some powerful moments, and I think we should explore what's holding you back in life. In love.

EJB: Why do you think anything is holding me back?

CHARLEY: Look here at *The Eight of Swords*. What do you feel?

EJ looked as she provided an image of the card on the screen for them both to look at. A figure stood blindfolded, bound, encircled by swords.

EJB: I want to help her. She's trapped, unhappy.

Charlotte sighed, staring at the screen. He was a

rescuer. She loved men with strong protective instincts; they were the knights, the real romantics. The heroes. Not that she personally needed rescuing, of course.

CHARLEY: Perhaps it would be worth talking about what inhibits you—what you are holding back, and why.

EJB: Maybe it means I'd like to be tied up and blindfolded.

CHARLEY: (laughing) That's always a possibility. Do you enjoy bondage?

EJB: I might, with the right person. I'm usually willing to try anything, once.

CHARLEY: I can see that—like we talked about last time, you're a very sensual man. You crave it—but you also want more. Something deeper, more meaningful. Does that sound right?

She was way off, but he wasn't about to let her know that. He was happy with his love life just the way it was, but he supposed she had a script of things she said to people to elicit certain responses. He was willing to play along.

EJB: I don't know. I enjoy women. I don't want to be tied down, but sometimes…

CHARLEY: Sometimes what?

EJB: I don't know. I date a lot, and I love a woman in my bed, but sometimes there is something missing. Sharing. Warmth, I guess.

He watched the words he'd typed pop up on the screen, almost without him thinking about it, and he stopped typing, sitting back, blinking. It was happening again. With almost no effort, she managed to get him to tell her private thoughts, things he barely admitted to himself.

CHARLEY: So you are a romantic at heart. I felt that. You have an active sex life; your body is being engaged, but not your heart.

EJB: Do you enjoy romance, Charley?

CHARLEY: I think all women do.

EJB: I want to know about you.

CHARLEY: Let's draw another card for you first. See what's coming your way in terms of romance, of something deeper than one-night stands.

EJ waited a beat as she expertly deflected the attention from herself; maybe this wasn't going to be as easy as he thought.

He saw another image pop up on the screen. The card didn't have any images on it, but displayed a group of sticks—what he knew now was the tarot suit of Wands—flying through the air, the Roman numeral VIII printed clearly at the top.

CHARLEY: *Eight of Wands*—fire, movement and change. This seems like a favorable indication of new opportunities coming your way, but there's some question about how well things will go, or if you are ready for what's about to happen.

EJB: You get all that from looking at one card with sticks flying through the air?

CHARLEY: (laughing) Well, I've talked with you a few times now, so I'm detecting patterns. And it's not all about the image itself. It's the suit, the number, the element the suit represents. In this case, fire. Swords, in your previous card, represent air—your intellectual side, your thoughts, the mind. So the issues are between mind and heart, rationality and desire.

Looking at it elementally, fire is fed by air—so your thoughts, what's going in inside your mind, are feeding these passions you feel, maybe in some form of dreams or wishes, but they're also holding you back, as the *Eight of Swords* indicated. You're being careful. Guarded. The question is why? What are you worried about?

The fact that both cards are eights is also important—numbers have lots of various interpretations, but in Chinese mythology this number is very auspicious, suggesting a time of growth and change, new beginnings. So I think you have a lot to look forward to, though it doesn't hurt to be careful. When we want something bad enough, we can be blind to the consequences.

EJ sat back, watching her analysis roll out on the screen, fascinated in spite of himself, and then quickly got a grip. This was the danger, that she could figure out what he needed to hear—that was the hook. And she was very good—however she arrived at her conclusions, or maybe it was in the delivery, she made him want to believe.

EJ decided the moment was right to push things a little further.

EJB: It feels good to talk with someone who understands. Who can see the things I need, what's inside.

CHARLEY: We all need that.

EJB: True, but I feel like we have a…connection. You have somehow managed to see things about me that even my closest friends don't know.

Charlotte sat back, looking warily at the words EJB typed in, unsure how to respond. It seemed like he was reading her mind, mirroring her thoughts. She'd been purposely trying to keep things less sexual tonight, concentrating on his deeper needs, his emotional situation, but even so, she still had this incredible feeling of electricity just talking to him. And apparently he felt it, too.

She knew it was breaking her own set of professional rules, but she followed her heart.

CHARLEY: I know. I've felt it, too. But it's not right for me to get personally involved with a client…

EJB: How could this not be personal? Everything we've shared has been personal. Intimate.

CHARLEY: I've just never had this happen before. It's very powerful.

Yeah, right. EJ rolled his eyes, ignoring his own increased heartbeat, telling himself it was just excitement at setting the trap while he tapped at the keys, playing out the conversation.

EJB: Me, either. But I feel like the change that the cards say is coming into my life is…you. Maybe the risk I'm supposed to take involves you.

CHARLEY: You really think so?

Charlotte's heart beat furiously, and her palms were actually sweating. On some level she'd known this was going to happen—there had just been something about their previous conversation that suggested it—but still, she couldn't believe it was really happening. It was so…*romantic*. She and this man she'd never met had a genuine, spiritual bond, and it was the most romantic thing she'd ever experienced. He wasn't like other men who were condescending about her spirituality or her tarot reading, or who approached sex as if it were a sport. EJB was sensitive, expressive and open.

EJB: What do the cards say?

She picked up her deck, and shuffled carefully, holding the deck close by her heart, feeling the cool breeze from the window against her overly warm skin as she cut the deck and took the card from the top, flipping it over slowly, hoping… *The Lovers*.

3

CHARLOTTE'S HEART leapt as she looked down at the nude figures intertwined in a passionate embrace even though she knew the cards were not literal—seeing the *Death* card didn't mean you were going to die, and seeing *The Lovers* didn't necessarily mean you were going to become romantically involved. But it didn't mean you weren't, either. It all depended on free will, and what she decided to do at this very critical moment. She could walk away, or she could take a chance.

She clicked the image so it appeared on the screen for EJB to see, too, not typing a word.

EJB: That's amazing.

CHARLEY: It can be about difficult situations, and making good choices. It's not always about romance.

EJB: Maybe we should choose to make it about romance.

CHARLEY: (smiling) I was kind of hoping you'd say that.

She let out a happy little squeak after she'd typed the words, bopping up and down and nearly knocking the laptop from its perch on her thighs. She was excited as all get out. Could this really be happening to her?

Thoughts raced through her mind. What did EJB look like? What was his voice like? What color were his eyes? He had to be handsome, with the active sex life he'd mentioned. She thought about that for a second, and shrugged. So what if he was a bit of a playboy? If she was going to try to have a romance, it might as well be with a man who knew what he was doing.

She wondered what his real name was. She had seen his credit card payment, but it just said his last name—Beaumont—and the first two initials. She wanted to know his first name, so she could see how it felt moving past her lips for the very first time.

EJB: Can we set the tarot cards aside for a few minutes and get to know each other a little bit?

CHARLEY: Okay. I was just thinking I wanted to know what your real first name was.

EJB: (smiling) I guess that's a good place to start. Actually, I usually go by my initials, EJ, since my dad, and my grandad, had the same first and middle names. But my full name is Ethan Jared Beaumont.

Charlotte pressed a hand to her heart, inhaling and then whispering the name on the breath she released. He even had a romantic name, for goodness sake. She said it over a few times, and then answered.

CHARLEY: May I call you Ethan?

EJB: I kind of prefer EJ, only because my dad was Ethan, and I'd rather hear my name than his off your beautiful lips. And I assume your real name is not Charley?

CHARLEY: No, but it's a shortened form of my real name, Charlotte.

EJB: That's beautiful—it's incredibly sexy. I've never known a woman with that name. Until you.

Charlotte felt herself blush, and rolled her eyes at herself. Oh, my.

CHARLEY: Thank you. What else would you like to talk about? I asked about names, so I guess it's your turn.

EJB: Personally, I'm wondering what you like in

bed. What your favorite spot to be touched is, what makes you cry out.

CHARLEY: I haven't had all that much experience finding out, I'm afraid to say. Does that bother you?

EJ scowled at the screen. What game was she playing now? He was supposed to be playing the dupe, letting himself appear to be reeled in, so he played along.

EJB: Are you saying you're a virgin?

CHARLEY: (laughing) No, not quite. But it's been a while. A long while.

EJB: Care to share why?

CHARLEY: Nothing earthshaking, just life. I had other priorities and, well, I don't make a habit out of having casual sex.

EJB: That's good to know. I can't say I've been serious with anyone in a while, either, though I'm open to the idea. With the right person. It's just that between running the family business and dealing with life, there hasn't been time to find her.

He sat back in his chair, smiling. That should bait the hook nicely. If she hadn't recognized his name already as part of one of Norfolk's leading families, she at least knew he was successful in some sense.

CHARLEY: Work can be rewarding, but it's hard to not let it take over your life and crowd out everything else.

EJB: True. I love my work, but I'm finding you to be quite the distraction. I was thinking about you all day at work today.

CHARLEY: You were? Why?

EJB: I guess it's the things you shared with me. The intimacy between us. We may not have had sex—yet—but we talked about it, and you've gotten under my skin.

CHARLEY: EJ… I don't know what to say.

EJB: Say you'll meet me.

CHARLEY: That may not actually be possible.

EJB: Where do you live?

CHARLEY: Virginia.

EJB: Where in Virginia?

CHARLEY: On the coast. Norfolk.

EJB: Charley, fate is on our side.

CHARLEY: Why do you say that?

EJB: I live in Norfolk, too.

Charlotte sat back, stunned. Was this possible? She'd heard a lot of stories about people meeting on the Internet, traveling incredible distances to be together, but ending up in the same city? She might not be so surprised in an enormous population like New York City, but for two people in Norfolk—the sheer magic of it floored her, and she had no idea what to say.

EJB: Charlotte. I'm sorry, I didn't mean to shock you. This is a huge coincidence, I know, but it's not all that uncommon these days. Maybe we're just lucky. Maybe it's fate. Are you okay?

CHARLEY: Not scared. Amazed.

EJ sighed—of course. Amazed because she believed she'd found yet another dupe to rob blind. He was surprised she hadn't backed off when he ended up living in the same town, and wanted to meet. Maybe Ian was right and she was just the in-formation gathering point for a larger operation, because he'd expected it would be safer for her to stay anonymous—unless she was angling for a bigger take.

If she'd checked out his registration information, and the credit card information from his donation, she would know a lot about him already. She'd know he lived in a wealthy neighborhood, and that he was in her backyard. He supposed she had to play it cool, pretend like she had no idea. She might know a lot of other things, depending on how good she was with a computer network.

He wanted to get to the bottom of this. Whatever was going on, Charlotte Gerard was part of it, and he wanted to find out how. No doubt they had other victims on the line, and he wanted to close this down before they took some other poor guy's life savings.

EJB: Charlotte, can you do another reading for me? In person.

CHARLEY: I'd love to, EJ. That would be perfect.

EJB: I understand your concerns, and we could meet in a public place, a café, if you like.

Charlotte sat back, considering. She knew that was the smart thing to do, but she didn't like the idea of meeting EJ with lots of people around, or reading for him in public, which was bound to be a very personal experience, considering.

Putting her faith in the universe, she flipped another card: *The Fool*. While she might be foolish to take such a leap, the card generally advised taking a chance, and trusting that things would work out. So she held her breath and took the plunge.

CHARLEY: No, I'd really rather meet you at your house.

She decided, ultimately, that it was safer to meet him at his place, so he didn't find out where she lived. Also, if the residence looked sketchy, she could just leave.

EJ: Thank you, Charlotte. I have a feeling this is going to be life-changing for both of us.

THE NEXT DAY, Charlotte stepped from the taxi, smoothing her yellow and white pinstriped seer-sucker sundress and catching her breath at the sight before her. It was the most beautiful house she'd ever seen, with the ivy-covered porch and bursts of spring flowers everywhere.

Its grandness could have been off-putting with the porch's sturdy columns and iron rails, but everything was wrapped in green and color, the plants were mature and well-tended. No modern landscaping could rival it. This gorgeous old house had known love, nurturing and happy times.

It must also be worth a fortune. She counted the beautiful, multi-paned windows on just the front—twenty-one. Wow. She looked up to the third floor, wondering what it would be like to gaze from one of those windows down on the magnolias that were just past their peak. The grass was green and lush, without a weed in sight. Relatively assured the man she was meeting was probably not an axe-murderer—not that money guaranteed against that, but she was willing to err on the side of her instincts—she waved to the taxi driver and sent him on his way with a smile.

Stepping up on the porch, she pushed the buzzer and waited, heart pounding. The man who would open the door had been sizzling in her fantasies for days, and now she was going to meet him face-to-face. Not one to succumb to nerves so easily, she was virtually vibrating with excitement and anticipation.

Nothing happened. No one arrived at the door. Pushing one curl, damp from the heat and plastered to her forehead, back in place, she hit the buzzer again, this time, holding it down longer, frowning.

Still nothing. Pursing her lips, she took a deep breath. She didn't believe EJ was the kind of man to stand her up—especially on the porch of his very own home. She decided to look out back.

Sure enough, as she rounded the end of a long,

curving drive, she spotted a man working in the yard and caught her breath again.

Oh my.

Standing atop a wooden ladder by the side of a large gazebo, he was stretched tall, wearing only low-slung jeans and a white T-shirt that clung, grooming the very fruitful wisteria that covered the panels of the charming structure. He must be the gardener—maybe he'd know where EJ was.

But Charlotte just stood there and watched for a moment. How could she do anything but? He was gorgeous. His muscles clenched and released as he maneuvered the clippers around the curves of the beautiful vine, taking care not to damage the huge, lavender-blue blossoms.

Watching him work told her more than the man would probably ever suspect. How he gently worked his way around the blossoms, how he made precise cuts.

Heat gathered low in her stomach, and she tried to control the flush that moved up into her cheeks as carnal images flashed through her mind. She was here to see one man, and getting all hot and bothered over another. She shook her head, surprised. It wasn't her habit to gawk, but as she let her eyes travel up the length of the man's taut form, resting for a few moments on his narrow, masculine hips and backside, she couldn't suppress a sharp twist of desire.

She was going to meet EJ looking flushed and bewildered, and she didn't want to be sending out the wrong signals. They'd acknowledged the spark between them online, and now they had to see if it would fade in real life. She knew she was there for much more than a reading—but if she thought about that too much she wouldn't be able to take one more step forward.

Time to stop ogling the gardener.

Gathering her composure, she stepped forward, a little more nervous than she had been. The grounds of the house were huge, and she walked slowly through the gorgeous yard where everything was blossoming, eager to burst from the bud. Her body felt heavy and warm the closer she got to the gazebo, and she pushed her hair back from her forehead again. Finally she stopped, trying to control her voice as she observed him close-up.

"Excuse me, I'm looking for EJ Beaumont. Could you tell me where to find him?" She wished her voice wasn't so breathless, but it was the best she could do.

The clipping stopped and the man turned slowly on the ladder, looking down at her with clear green eyes that warmed as he looked at her. His gaze was as lush as the foliage surrounding him, and she couldn't look away.

"Charlotte." Her name escaped from his lips on a husky welcome, his genteel southern drawl softening the consonants and making it sound much more romantic than she'd ever thought it was.

"EJ?" Her voice was barely a whisper. Oh. My. God. The gardener was EJ?

He didn't step down from the ladder right away, but stayed there, towering above her, taking her in as if he never wanted to stop looking at her. He didn't say another word, and she started to feel like a bug under a microscope. But then he smiled.

She double-stepped a little, thinking she'd hit an uneven patch in the yard. Either that or this was the first time in her life a man's smile had literally tipped her off balance. She looked up, dazed, and he smiled even more widely, starting down the ladder.

"Charlotte," he repeated, as if feeling her name with his mouth, melting her knees in the process. She almost backed up a step, mesmerized and trying to escape his spell, clearly in over her head. But she held her ground, waiting.

She opened her mouth but no sound came out as he walked up close, and took both of her hands in his. His skin was warm from his work, his hands rough but not calloused, his touch welcoming but not inappropriate. Curling her fingers around his was the most natural move in the world, and she lifted her eyes and fell into heaven.

"EJ," she said again. "Oh. I thought you were the gardener." She swallowed, catching her breath. "I'm sorry. I mean, I'm not sorry you're the gardener—that's a fine profession and I love gardens, but I am a little early, I have this thing about time, I like to be on time, I hate to be late, so I end up being early all the time, but being early can be just as rude as being late, but…"

She ended her babble, staring haplessly, watching him nod slowly and seriously as if every word coming out of her mouth made absolute sense.

She felt a rush of disbelief and confusion. How could this amazingly hot…*stud*—it was the only word she could think of—not be taken? How could he not have the woman of his choice in his bed every night? What was he doing getting tarot readings online and standing here with *her*?

Chasing away the self-denigrating thought, she smiled and looked around the yard, trying to ignore the fact that he was still holding onto her hands.

"I'm not the gardener, Charlotte, I just like to work outside from time to time. This is my family home, though I'm the only one who lives here now. With my work, I spend a lot of time inside at a desk, so I try to get outdoors and do things when I get the opportunity."

"Your home is gorgeous. I've never seen wisteria that prolific." Thank God, she managed to say something halfway intelligent that time. She even sounded normal.

"Really?" He glanced back and then returned his gaze to her. "It's hard to keep it from invading, actually. This one is almost fifteen years old, and we have to make sure we don't let it take over the yard."

"Oh. We?" she asked vaguely, still looking into his handsome face. His mouth was firm and straight—he had nice, manly lips, not too full, but a perfect complement to his slightly sharpened cheekbones, tanned skin and sandy hair. Spontaneously combusting from the inside out, she wondered what he would taste like.

"Well, it's just me now. I used to work out here with my mother quite a bit, but she moved shortly after my father died."

"Oh, I'm sorry to hear you lost your father."

"Thanks, but it's been years. Mom's seeing someone new, even."

"Oh." He was so close his scent permeated her space—ginger, moss and earthy, delicious man—and she closed her eyes, letting it envelop her.

"Are you okay?"

Her eyes flew open quickly—she'd completely forgotten herself. My God, the man had her in a swoon! She almost giggled, feeling uncharacteristically light, excited, and buzzing like one of the bees on the flowers.

"I'm fine. I was just getting a good vibe, is all."

"You're from New England."

"Yes, New Hampshire."

"It's beautiful there. I like your accent."

She laughed then, forgetting how different she sounded here until someone mentioned it. "Thanks. New England is great, but I like it much better here. I like the sun and the warmth."

As if on cue, her face flushed once more when he stroked a thumb absently—or purposefully—over her palm before letting her fingers go. His eyes had darkened a shade to the most stunning jade she'd ever seen. None of this seemed real, including EJ.

"Let me wash up and we can get to know each other a little. You did bring your cards?"

"Oh, yes, they're in my bag."

"Let's go inside. I'm looking forward to this."

Charlotte thought, following behind as he led the way, that saying she felt the same way would be a radical understatement.

EJ HAD RARELY been rendered speechless in his lifetime, but he was just glad he'd been able to get his wits about him as quickly as he did. When he'd heard the soft female voice speak to him and turned to find *her* standing there, he'd almost fallen from the ladder.

He wasn't expecting her early, and he wasn't expecting…he wasn't sure. To feel so bowled over, maybe. But the real Charlotte was very different than the pictures in her file. She packed a wallop up close.

The image of her standing, looking up at him on the ladder, was burnt into his mind. If he'd known how beautiful she was, their online chat would have brought him to his knees. Baby-soft looking blond curls flew everywhere in charming disarray, framing what could only be described as an angelic face, with a petite nose, doe-brown eyes, and petal-pink lips that had him sweating with the effort to stem his body's visceral response.

But it was too late—he could imagine that sweet, moist mouth wrapped around him, sending him sky-rocketing into pleasure. He adjusted his gardening belt to hide the result of that momentary flight of fancy.

Charlotte was petite, the top of her head only coming to his mid-chest, but she wasn't slight or dainty—supple and lush were probably better terms. She wore no makeup that he could see, no stockings, and just a simple silver chain around her wrist. He wondered what she wore under that dress, if any-thing.

The light yellow shift didn't accentuate her curves, but hugged her breasts and butt enticingly as he slowed down and let her move ahead of him. Those huge brown eyes took in everything, thanking him quietly when he held the door for her and let her in the back door, to the kitchen. She wore thick, chunky sandals, and her toenails were painted with clear polish. She looked…earthy. Sensual, but innocent.

But EJ knew she wasn't. Even if she wasn't a thief, she was connected to the scam somehow. And how she'd talked to him about his sex life indicated she was far from inexperienced and pure—though that didn't make it easier to calm his reactions. It would be to her benefit to look innocent, seductive—

he had to remember she was on the make. And he was fighting the urge to be a willing victim. Hell, she hadn't needed to rob people online—if she'd met those men in person, they probably would gladly give her anything she wanted.

Which made him wonder what she wanted, what she liked.

Trying to sound casual, he poured her a glass of lemonade and excused himself to change. He hoped to find some shred of self-control in the process.

"I'll just be a minute," he said, smiling as he handed her the glass. "Make yourself comfortable, feel free to look around."

Leaving before she could even acknowledge him, he took a deep breath and hopped the stairs two at a time to his room. Ducking into a quick, rinsing shower, he dried off and found a clean pair of pants and a decent shirt. He hoped Charlotte did show herself around.

He wanted to make himself an irresistible target, to sweeten the pot so that she couldn't resist. He'd even left a checkbook—not his real one, of course— sitting innocuously on the counter, waiting for inquiring eyes to investigate and perhaps memorize his account number. Baiting the trap.

When he hit the bottom of the stairs, his stomach clenched nonetheless when he saw her holding his grandmother's music box.

"It's an antique from the 1800s. My grandfather

had it made for my grandmother for their wedding, and it is passed on when each son or daughter marries. It will go to my sister, Grace, if she ever decides to marry, and if not, to my wife. Should I ever marry, as well."

She smiled, setting it down carefully. "It's gorgeous. It must be so nice to have that kind of family history, things that are passed down from one person to another."

"Doesn't your family pass things down?"

He felt a little stab of guilt saying that, knowing what he knew about her past—there'd been no family, let alone family heirlooms for Charlotte Gerard—but he wasn't supposed to know that. After a slight shadow passed over her face, she brightened again.

"No, not before. I didn't know my parents. But for me, maybe in the future there will be children, if the situation is right. And I'd love to have things to pass along, though nothing this beautiful, I'm sure."

He stepped closer, reaching down to touch the smooth mahogany box and looking at her reassuringly. "It's not about the price of the item. It's about who had it before. That's what makes heirlooms important. Every time I play this, I think of my grandmother. And I remember how my grandfather loved her."

Charlotte was gazing up at him with every hopeful thought shining in her eyes, and she looked like the least likely thief he'd ever met. Clearing his throat, a bit unsettled at the open adoration in her expression, he gestured to the table.

"Do you still want to do a reading for me?"

"Absolutely."

Was that light in her eyes due to the undeniable sexual attraction between them or excitement over finding such easy pickings? EJ smiled, walking closely by her side and trying to remember she was a suspect, even though her sexy scent was criminal in an entirely different way.

"Do you have any preference where you read?"

She shrugged. "Not really. A table is nice, and if I can get a north-facing chair, even better, but I read cards just about anywhere."

EJ opted not to ask about the north-facing chair issue but showed her to the sunny kitchen table and watched her sit, leaning over to retrieve the cards from her bag, and he couldn't stop himself from admiring the generous cleavage the move exposed.

He'd always preferred smaller women with streamlined builds—compact, but feminine. However, he found himself imagining what it would be like to weigh the roundness of Charlotte's breasts in his palms, to nestle his face in the warmth of all that fullness. The thought nearly paralyzed him with need. He blinked, realizing she'd said something to him. He didn't hear the words, but he zeroed in on the movement of those delicious lips.

"I'm sorry, what?"

She smiled, and a bright pink stain bloomed in her cheeks. No surprise, he probably hadn't been very discreet about his leering. She didn't seem offended, in fact, a pleased sparkle danced in those deep brown irises.

A touch of cynicism straightened his back—of course she didn't mind. She was probably thrilled that he was so easy to lure in, to distract. That he was so obviously lusting after her. She looked through the deck quickly, pulling out a card and placing it in front of him, face up.

"*The King of Pentacles*. This is your significator."

"What does that mean?"

"It's just a representation of you. Who you are in the reading. Kings are usually used to represent mature males. At first, only knowing you online, I would have been tempted to choose the *King of Wands* or *Cups*, but seeing you here, in your home and in the gardens, I can't help but choose pentacles."

"If you say so."

EJ didn't miss the symbolism; maybe Charlotte was giving away too much through her selection of cards without realizing it. Though nature was a prominent element in the image on the card, the figure sat upon a throne and was blanketed with riches. Not very subtle, actually; it was clear how *she* was seeing him.

Maybe there was something to be said for this tarot business. He studied the card more closely, seemingly unaware of her watching him, when in reality he was attuned to her every breath, her every move.

"Just focus on the significator and your question while I shuffle."

"Shouldn't we hold hands or something?"

She smiled patiently. "That's for a séance. We're fine as we are—I couldn't shuffle the deck if we held hands. Focus, now."

He obeyed her gentle command, feeling foolish and intrigued at the same time. She seemed to really be into it. She put the cards in front of him and asked him to cut them into three piles then recombine them. He did so, and waited as she asked for his question and started to turn out cards.

Her soft voice was almost hypnotic as she spun a story from card to card, stopping to check for clarifications or his input, answering his questions and showing him what the puzzle laid out in front of him meant. By the end of the reading, he was more than confused. He was completely unsettled, but also fascinated.

How deeply had this woman studied his life? How much information had she managed to get about him before she came to his door? It had to be considerable, since her "reading" was uncannily accurate. If she was working alone, she had to have connections. But more likely, she really was the front person. She checked potential targets out, set them up, and then someone else did the real dirty work.

And she'd also take the fall if something went down—if the operation closed up shop and disappeared, she'd be the only one left hanging in the wind. The thought disturbed him, and he tried to squelch his protective feelings. She was in this up to her pretty little mouth, and he shouldn't be sympathizing. And the way she'd stimulated some of his more male responses had him wondering if he was losing his grip when it came to this case. He tried to refocus, to get back in the game.

How could she know, if she hadn't checked him out, about the friends in his life who were getting married or having children? How could she know about his professional success and his old relationships? All of that was something any enterprising person could find out with phone calls, newspaper research and good old legwork.

In spite of the falsified information he'd included in his registration, and dummy documents anyone would find if they used the artificial papers, she kept returning to his role as a "protector"—did she know he was a cop? The thought niggled at him, but then he relaxed. If she knew he was a cop, she would have never shown up. She probably knew about his family's shipbuilding plant, but Beaumont Industries wasn't exactly a secret.

"So it's been a bumpy road, some ups and downs, but you've made some good choices recently. Your professional life seems like it has blessings everywhere—you are very happy in your work, though frustrated in other areas of your life."

"That's true. I value my job, and what it allows me to do for the community."

"What do you do?"

"My family owns Beaumont Industries. Have you heard of it?"

She shook her head—the little liar.

"I've only been here a few years, and I don't really read newspapers or anything like that."

Yeah, right.

"We own one of the largest and oldest shipbuilding plants in the area. My great-grandfather started the business, and built one of the first tugboats. It's still on display in the local naval museum."

"That's just incredible! I'd love to see it."

"I'll take you."

She blushed again, and EJ just couldn't help but respond to how pretty she was. If only she weren't a fraud.

"What do you do with the company? You mentioned helping the community?"

"We donate to causes, sponsor events, provide a significant number of local jobs and we are an environmentally safe industry. My father didn't wait for the laws to force compliance. He cared about the natural world, and he taught us to, as well."

"I could tell from the grounds of this house. It's like a paradise."

EJ watched her and felt stymied again. She looked so earnest. She didn't press him for more details on his work, or anything else suspicious. That made him doubly cautious—she was either completely innocent or she was very good.

He intended to find out.

4

CHARLOTTE WAS CONVINCED AS she turned out the cards and read for EJ that there was something special and unusual between them. Sparks flew each time they caught each other's eyes, and she was having a hard time separating her professional responsibilities from her personal desires. She didn't want to make him uncomfortable, and she owed him her best insights, but the cards and the reading had gotten increasingly focused on relationships, on passion, and the heat was almost tangibly building between them in the room.

Turning the last card, *The Star*, she felt marginally better—this card was a blessing, a positive omen for things turning out well. When she looked up again, she saw EJ closely studying the card which displayed a nude woman among the sun and stars, a pitcher in each hand.

"She reminds me of you." EJ's voice was low and full of sexual promise, and she couldn't take her eyes off the card as he continued to study the image. "She's so sensual."

She'd brought her Morgan-Greer deck, her favorite, because the images were so colorful and lush. As she looked down at *The Star*, she realized he was right, though her hair was curlier than the woman's on the card. However, the exposed body of the image made her feel exposed as well, the rosy tips of the woman's breasts suddenly felt like her own. The way EJ was looking at her made her own nipples tingle in response.

"I'm a little heavier."

"You're more beautiful."

She had no idea what to say. The casual back and forth of the tarot reading had swerved in a new direction, and she swallowed, unsure how to react. Reflexively, she reached forward, starting to gather up the cards, and his hands trapped hers gently.

"Don't leave yet. We've only started." His gaze burned into her. "I want to spend more time with you."

"I want to spend more time with you, too, but I have dog-walking appointments."

"I thought you read tarot for a living?"

"No, that's one thing I do, but I have several odd jobs that keep the rent paid. So I really do have to go."

She wasn't afraid of EJ; she just had a swell of emotion she didn't understand overtake her, and she felt like she couldn't breathe, the suggestion had become so thick between them.

He crossed to her side of the table, letting go of one of her hands but keeping hold of the other. Kneeling down by the side of her chair, he looked concerned.

"I'm sorry, Charlotte. I didn't mean to come on so strong, but having you here in person ties me in knots. I don't know what I expected, but I didn't expect to feel everything that I do."

Charlotte melted at his confession, her panic easing as she looked into his beautiful face.

"I'm sorry. I just have never…I don't know how to respond to you. To this."

He leaned in, his face close to hers, his free hand sliding up into her hair. "I'm betting you know exactly how to respond."

All she could do was make a tiny "mmm" sound before his mouth claimed hers, and it was hardly a protest. She forgot everything as his lips touched hers in an exploratory kiss. It was the kind of kiss she'd never experienced and had always dreamt of, and her doubts evaporated as if they'd never existed.

His hand stayed on the back of her head, angling her so he could widen her lips and access her mouth more effectively, tasting her as if she were living, breathing ambrosia. She sighed into his mouth, letting her tongue touch his and moaning at the power of the tentative touch.

Just as she felt like she could sink into the kiss forever and never let it end, he pulled back, his eyes dark with desire, his breath coming slightly faster.

The idea that she'd excited him so was unbelievable to her, but the pulse pounding at the base of his neck convinced her. She leaned forward slightly, wanting to kiss him in that spot, to feel the throbbing beneath his skin against her mouth. But then he spoke, halting her impulse.

"I want to take you out. To dinner. On a date. Though right now I'd like to peel that dress off of you and taste every inch of you, my mama raised a gentleman. We should get to know each other a little. First."

The not-so-veiled heat in his expression and the seductive promise of his words pushed another flush up into her cheeks as she answered. "I'd like that."

Imagine. A man who actually wanted to take her out, not just take her to bed.

He smiled, lifting his hand and rubbing her moist lower lip with his thumb. "How about the Isle, at the wharf? Tomorrow at seven? I'll pick you up."

Her eyes widened. The Isle was one of the most prestigious restaurants in the area. She'd never even dreamed of going to a place like that, but the prospect of being taken there by EJ was too magical to resist.

"Okay, but you don't have to pick me up—I'd rather get there on my own, I have a lot going on in the afternoon, and will just be anxious if you show up and I'm not ready."

While that was partially true, she also realized, unhappily, that she didn't want to tell him where she lived, especially now that she'd had a glimpse of his life. Maybe he would change his mind. Maybe his opinion of her would change. She wanted the fantasy this time, and pushed the reality away just a little bit.

"Modern women," he sighed with comical exaggeration. "Okay, but I wish you would let me come get you. You could call me when you're ready."

"No, really, I'll be fine."

"If you insist, but I'll see you home and I don't want one word of argument about it."

He dipped closer to seal the date with another kiss, effectively quieting any objections she might have raised and erasing any more doubts before they had a chance to surface.

EJ LEVELED THE GUN and aimed at his target, the black silhouette of a human body hanging about one hundred feet in front of him. The weight of the .45 was reassuring in his hand. This was his favorite gun, and he tried to get to the range to shoot at least once a week, keeping his skills honed.

While some manufacturers were advocating virtual shooting ranges now, EJ liked to know he could handle the real thing, and smiled when he pulled the trigger, feeling the kick against his palms. The shot was a little off, but not bad. He tried again, relishing the power and the control that target shooting offered him. Like sex, shooting a gun wasn't something he ever wanted to do virtually. He preferred the real thing.

Bracing his legs, straightening his back, he started to pull the trigger when the tiny alarm from his PDA went off, reminding him that he had to get ready for his date.

A flash of Charlotte's features, the memory of the soft texture of her hair in his hand distracted him, making his next shot even farther off the mark.

Unacceptable. And definitely not healthy in his line of work.

But as his traitorous thoughts brought him back to the kiss, he set the gun down on the shelf in front of him, shaking his head and taking a moment to regroup. He'd been pushing the thoughts aside all day, refusing to accept what had happened as more than part of the job, setting up the sting to catch Charlotte Gerard in the act, but his gut was telling him an entirely different story.

Or was it just rampant lust? Normally he would trust his instincts. He knew their evidence suggested that Charlotte was the guilty party, but his instincts were compelling him to think more about kissing her again than arresting her. Though snapping handcuffs around those delicate wrists presented some definite possibilities....

Blood traveled straight to his groin at the thought, and he took a deep breath, looking from side to side, making sure he was alone. It was embarrassing, how much he wanted her. Anyone would think he hadn't been laid in a while, which wasn't the problem at all.

But Charlotte had packed a punch to his libido, and he wasn't sure what to do about it.

She was a stranger—a prime suspect—and it had been all he could do not to peel away that cute little sundress and ravish every inch of her curvy flesh. He'd done some deeper digging after she left, hoping to find something that would condemn her and cool his lust, but there was nothing.

He wanted to see where she lived. How she lived. That was the next priority. If she liked furniture she couldn't afford, or if he found anything that would give him a sense of her having more money than she should, he would get his answers.

He rarely went to the Isle. It was just too uptight for his usual tastes. But Charlotte had seemed thrilled. She obviously had a yen for the finer things. But she'd been reluctant to let him come pick her up. It didn't add up—what was she hiding?

She wouldn't have the same success when it came to taking her home. Not only would the detective in him not be thwarted, but the gentleman in him would not accept leaving a woman at her doorstep alone late at night. And, if he was blunt, the man in him wanted to taste her again. For all the women he'd seen over the last few years, he couldn't recall such sharp anticipation of kissing his date good-night.

His thoughts whirled in confusion. He reminded himself she wasn't a date; she wasn't a potential lover. She was, potentially, a criminal. He had to remember that; he had no idea what lay beneath the surface of these thefts, and losing sight of that could cost him his life. Computer crime was usually fought on both fronts—behind a screen and behind a gun. He had to be prepared for that, no matter how much his dick insisted otherwise when it came to Charlotte.

With that sobering thought, he picked up his gun again, clearing his mind and taking a breath before snapping off five more shots in a row, hitting the target in five fatal areas.

Much better. Now he could go get ready for his date.

THE THRIFT SHOP at the community center downtown was her only hope. She had nothing to wear to a place like the Isle, and even in thrift-shop terms she wasn't planning to spend half her rent and hoped she could make it up before the end of the month. Still, she felt like Cinderella getting ready for the ball as she walked in and went directly toward the rack of formal dresses in the back. She needed something special.

The clerk, a petite, twentysomething woman with short, dark hair looking bored to tears, approached her.

"Can I help you?"

Charlotte grimaced, not seeing anything particularly appropriate on the rack.

"I need a dress for a special event. Something really spectacular."

The clerk nodded, but eyed the rack with a frown. "It's coming up on prom season, the dresses are picked over."

"Do you have anything in the back?"

The young woman looked at her, as if lost in thought, and Charlotte pushed, "I really need a dress and I can't afford retail. I met a guy, and he's wonderful, but he invited me to dinner at the Isle, and I don't have anything—it's tonight, so I can't go all over the city looking. Are you sure all the formal dresses are gone?"

"Wow, the Isle? This must be some guy." The clerk was obviously impressed and Charlotte grinned proudly.

"He is. He's so-oo-o handsome, I can barely believe he asked me out. I just met him, and I don't want to show up looking like a ragamuffin, but money is tight."

"I hear ya, hon. Listen—" she pursed her lips thoughtfully "—there is a dress in the back. You are, what, about a size ten?"

"Depends on the cut, but yeah, in that range."

"Give me a minute. I think this was an eight, but it was a loose cut, so we can try it."

Charlotte waited, her anxiety levels rising as the clerk didn't return, and she wondered what she would do if she couldn't find a dress. She had some dresses, but nothing formal enough for the Isle. She could cancel, but how would that look?

EJ was like a prince, and that he wanted to take her on a fancy date was like a dream. A once-in-a-lifetime fantasy. She didn't want to miss it because she had nothing to wear. But she had dog-walking appointments in an hour, and she needed time to get showered and dressed. If this dress didn't fit, she was sunk.

Just as she was about to crawl out of her skin, the clerk emerged, holding a dress over her arm that left Charlotte speechless.

The clerk smiled, holding it up for inspection, and both women simply stared, glorying in the beautiful garment. The bias-cut gown, black French cotton lace draped over a golden silk charmeuse lining, was perfect. The cut was simple, but the effect of the design was exquisite. Charlotte reached out to touch it, almost afraid to.

"It's from some vintage designer. The owner of the shop told me, but I can't recall—Imelda? Isadora? I can never remember those names." She flipped the tag inside and smiled. "Isadora. Sharon, the owner, says it sells retail for over a thousand dollars! She wants to auction it on eBay, but the woman who left it specifically said she just wanted someone to have it who couldn't otherwise afford it so—"

The clerk lowered her voice, and looked from side to side before speaking again. "You seem nice, and going to the Isle is a big deal. If you want to take it just for your dinner and drop it back later, Sharon is out of town. She won't even notice if the dress is gone for one night. Just don't, you know, drop ketchup on it or anything. If the Isle even uses ketchup." The girl smiled, holding out her hand. "I'm Phoebe, by the way."

Charlotte was stunned and immediately shook her head.

"Hi, Phoebe. I'm Charlotte. You are really so generous, but I couldn't do that. It doesn't seem right. Whatever I get, I should pay for."

"Well, okay. Listen," she continued, her eyes sparkling conspiratorially. "Try it on. If you like it, then take it. Come back tomorrow morning around eight, when I open up, and we'll just put it back on the shelf, and you can make a donation to the shop—consider it a rental fee. As long as the dress comes back in one piece, what's the harm?"

Charlotte knew she was being somewhat happily steamrolled, but agreed to at least try on the dress. When Phoebe handed it to her, she ran her fingers over the sensuous textures of the silk and delicate lace, and knew she was done for.

In the tiny dressing room, she slid the silk over her head and sighed with pleasure when it fell down around her body, hanging at just the right height, hugging where it should. It draped beautifully, and Charlotte turned once, loving how forgiving the dress was of her less than perfect spots. It made her feel sexier than she ever thought she could.

The golden lining complemented her skin tone

and hair, making the dress elegantly sexual by creating the illusion of the black French lace draping over bare skin. She knew she had to wear this dress for EJ. Maybe it was the accumulation of some good karma that she'd found it, and that Phoebe was willing to break the rules for her a little bit, but she knew this was the perfect dress.

"Come out—I want to see. Does it fit?"

Charlotte couldn't contain her smile when she walked out through the creaky louvered door, delighting in Phoebe's slack-jawed reaction when she saw her.

"Oh, my God you're gorgeous! That dress was made for you." Her eyes widened and in her excitement, she completely ignored another customer who was trying to get her attention. "Oh! Wait! I have the perfect shoes!"

Charlotte smiled weakly at the ignored woman, shrugging. The older, black woman shook her head, looking after Phoebe, but then turned her assessing gaze back to Charlotte.

"You sure can wear that dress, girlfriend. My days of ever fitting in something like that are long gone, but you want to bring your man to his knees, that dress'll do it."

Charlotte remained speechless for a second, picturing EJ on his knees, then collapsed in giggles, laughing joyfully with the woman, who waited as Phoebe returned with several pairs of shoes. Both women passed opinions on which ones worked for her.

After modeling several pair, they all decided on a pair of simple but deadly black pumps, and Charlotte hoped she'd have time to stop at the store and find a black velvet ribbon for her hair. She brought her purchases to the counter, suddenly apprehensive again.

"You're sure you want to do this? I want to pay for the shoes."

Phoebe rolled her eyes in the way only hip, twenty-something women can and waved away Charlotte's apprehension. "I want you to wear this dress tonight—and share all the details with me tomorrow."

"Deal. And not only will I give you a donation tomorrow, but would you like a tarot card reading as well? I read cards professionally."

"Get out! That's so cool! I've always wanted a tarot reading. Can you do it when you come back?"

"Absolutely—but it might be later in the morning, if that's okay? I have dog-walking appointments in the morning."

"No problem. I'm here all day, and Sharon's gone for two more days. And what she doesn't know won't hurt her. She shouldn't be trying to make more of a profit off this dress as it is."

"Well, she probably is just trying to do what's best for the shop."

Phoebe rang up the shoes, and took Charlotte's money. "I suppose. But still, the woman who gave it to us would love that you are wearing it tonight, I just know it. She really wanted someone to get to enjoy the dress."

Charlotte smiled, liking that the previous owner of the beautiful dress was such a generous person.

"I'll see you tomorrow, Phoebe. And I promise to be careful with the ketchup."

EJ LOOKED AT HIS WATCH, wondering if he was being stood up. Perusing the small, elegant dining room, he wondered if he'd pushed too hard, come on too strong and frightened Charlotte away. He never really thought about it, but as his eyes traveled over the snow-white tablecloths, the glistening flatware, perfect china plates and bunches of perfect pink roses on every table, he could imagine how such an atmosphere could be intimidating to someone who wasn't used to it.

Or had Charlotte been spooked for another reason? Was she worried he was getting too close to figuring out her secret?

It hadn't been difficult getting a table—his mother was a regular diner here, and the Beaumont name carried some weight—but he'd been sitting alone for twenty minutes now. He'd give it ten more minutes before—

He stopped thinking. He stopped breathing altogether when she was escorted into the room by the maitre d'.

Stunning. Sexy. Breathtaking. Holy shit, he was in trouble.

She smiled tentatively, walking slowly to the table, a vision in black lace and satin, her lovely curls tied up in a softly flowing black ribbon. She still wore no makeup, no jewelry, though her cheeks burst with color as his gaze held hers, and her lips…her lips were as luscious and tempting as ever. He found himself licking his own, taking a deep breath and standing to take her hand as she approached the table. Even if she was a suspect, she was a beautiful woman, and he couldn't—and didn't want to—ignore his response to her. At least for the moment.

"Charlotte." He let his eyes travel the entire length of her, taking in every inch of the gorgeous dress until she warmed beneath his gaze, the buds of her breasts blossoming under the fabric that caressed them.

"You are stunning. That dress is exquisite." And if he wasn't mistaken, a very expensive designer garment. He didn't know a lot about specific designers, but he'd grown up with two women in the house, and he knew quality when he saw it.

"Thank you. I'm sorry I'm late. My taxi was caught in traffic."

EJ frowned. "I should have picked you up. I apologize."

"No, this is fine. I had such a busy day, is all." She looked around, taking in her surroundings as he pulled out her chair and she sat. "This place is…incredible. The view alone is worth paying for."

As she turned to look out the wall of clear glass overlooking the Bay and the twinkling lights of the bridge, he leaned in, inhaling her natural feminine scent and placed a light kiss on her neck. He was close enough to feel her breath catch, and to see her full breasts rise beneath the low neckline of the gown.

It'd been many decades since he'd caught himself looking down a woman's dress—the last time was at a cousin's wedding, and he'd been fourteen and perpetually horny, and lucky enough to have sat next to a particularly well-endowed bridesmaid. He didn't feel so differently now, really, as he tried to drag his eyes away. Returning to his own chair, he poured them both champagne, and smiled, lifting his glass.

"To unexpected pleasures, made sweeter by their surprise."

She lifted her glass and touched it lightly to his, sipping the champagne with such savoring grace that he almost forgot to take a drink himself, content just to watch her.

What the heck was into him? He loved women—and he'd *loved* women—but it was almost like he was under a spell with Charlotte. Usually he was calm and collected, charming and discreet. But at the moment it was all he could do to breathe normally and not drag her off and see what was underneath that dress.

Getting his thoughts under control, he set his glass down without drinking any more, and smiled.

"So I want to know more about you, Charlotte."

"There's not much to tell, I'm afraid."

"Oh, I don't believe that. But with your readings and your visit to my home, I feel at a disadvantage—you know a lot about me, and I know next to nothing about you."

Lies, of course. He knew most of the surface details of her life, but he found himself curious about how much she would share, and what else might be underneath the surface.

Charlotte looked relieved when a waiter appeared. In spite of her independent, "I'll drive myself" approach to coming to the restaurant, she seemed more than happy to hand over the responsibility of ordering their food to him. Not that he minded, and ordered an extravagant, romantic meal.

"I hope you don't mind ordering—not having been here before, I didn't know what would be best."

"No problem at all. It's a gentleman's duty." He smiled and watched her eyes light up. She had a compelling natural beauty, and he was glad to be spending this time with her, whether it was professional of him to enjoy it so much or not.

"This is like a fairy tale. I feel like if I blink, it will all go away."

EJ was charmed in spite of himself, and he reached over the small table, capturing her hand in his.

"I'm glad you're enjoying yourself. You'll love the food—it's some of the best in the region."

"I don't usually eat meats or refined sugars, but tonight I am going to love whatever they serve, I just know it."

EJ didn't know about her eating habits—case files only went so far—but he was glad he'd ordered mostly seafood and pasta dishes, with beautiful salads. That was his preference as well.

"Are you a vegan?"

She laughed, and it was a great laugh. "Oh, no way. I'm not that disciplined. I love food, but I just try to stay away from red meats and sugars, though I do have a chocolate habit I can't quite conquer. I never had too much of it as a kid, and I have a hard time not overindulging now."

"Chocolate should be a basic food group. Did your family not believe in eating many sweets?"

"I didn't know my real family. My brother and I were given up, and grew up in group and foster homes, separately. Sometimes I got a birthday cake, but I think I got so tired of the salty processed foods that were standard fare at the group homes that once I was out on my own, I decided never to eat any of that again."

"But you still have a sweet tooth?"

"You bet. When I was free to buy my own food, and I discovered Häagen-Dazs, and good, dark chocolate, I thought I'd gone to heaven. I have to hold myself back, or I wouldn't fit through a doorway."

EJ regarded her curves appreciatively. "I think you're perfect. Bony is not sexy, in spite of what the media says."

She blushed, fidgeting awkwardly with her utensils, and didn't respond.

"So you mentioned a brother—a twin?"

"Oh, no. He's younger, but was given up to a different family before I even knew about him."

Charlotte took off telling him about her search for her brother. After she had discovered his existence while working part-time in one of the group-home offices, she'd pursued his whereabouts with dogged determination, from the sounds of it. She spoke matter-of-factly, as if anyone would—or could—have done what she did, but EJ knew differently. She'd had to use considerable resources of her own, not to mention the sheer will to persevere and locate a missing family member. He couldn't help but be impressed.

Their food arrived while she spoke, and the conversation continued pleasantly until they were ready for dessert. EJ had enjoyed the dinner immensely— Charlotte was a fascinating companion, but unfortunately she hadn't divulged any information that would make him suspect her more strongly. Unless she'd been running rackets to fund her family searches, but somehow he doubted it.

He was finding it more and more difficult to suspect her of anything, and wasn't sure how to proceed.

Or was he just rationalizing because she turned him on and he wanted to follow through on his desires with a clear conscience?

And he'd be less than honest with himself if he didn't admit that he just wanted to get Charlotte alone. She was a suspect, and he was a cop—but he was also a man. A very, very tempted man.

"Do you want dessert?"

She looked at him, and he saw the muted desire in her gaze, but it wasn't for dessert. Oh, man.

"Actually, I'm stuffed. This was wonderful, though I think the champagne went to my head a little."

"All part of my evil plan to get you to let me kiss you again."

The words popped out, but they were the truth. Obviously, his desires were winning out over his rational thinking.

"I don't think you needed the champagne for that, EJ."

He stood, pulling her up to stand closely in front of him, staring down into her liquid brown eyes. "Will you let me take you home?"

She just nodded, promises and hopes shining in her eyes as she looked up at him, and he felt as close to being a cad as he ever had in his life.

He paid the bill and escorted her from the restaurant. She was smiling so much by the time they hit the door he had to smile back.

"What's funny?"

"Oh, nothing. I wasn't smiling because I thought something was funny."

"Then what?"

They walked out the massive door and EJ signaled the valet to get his car. He stood close to Charlotte, leaning down to whisper in her ear. "You can tell me. Did I walk away with my napkin stuck to my shoe or spinach in my teeth?"

She laughed again, and held him with a look so potent he couldn't break it.

"No, it was just, well…this has been perfect. More than perfect. Dressing up, coming to a place like this, then walking out with my arm through yours, with everyone seeing us…it was…fun. Magical. I never experienced anything like that."

She'd never felt what it was like to dress up and go out, to have a man escort her from a restaurant? EJ would have responded, but he was stunned silent. She shook her head, looking down.

"I know it's stupid, but—"

He tipped her face up, staring into her eyes, forgetting for the moment what the reality between them was.

"No, not stupid. Not stupid at all. I'm…honored to be your date tonight, Charlotte."

"EJ, I…"

They were interrupted when his car arrived, a shining black BMW that made Charlotte's eyes widen into great pools. She didn't bother hiding that she was impressed. The valet opened the door, and EJ helped her into the passenger's seat. He leaned down to pull the seat belt over her, an excuse to get closer and brush her lips with a slight kiss.

"You amaze me, Charlotte. I've loved talking with you and getting to know you. But will you forgive me, darlin', for saying that all I can think about right now is getting you alone and out of that amazing dress?"

5

CHARLOTTE SANK INTO THE supple, deep leather of the form-fitting seat as the BMW sped quickly down the highway, guided by EJ's sure hand. The closeness of his body next to hers when he'd buckled her seat belt, the slight kiss he'd offered, and that whopper of a question he'd popped right before closing the door on her side had her mind in a whirl.

The girl who didn't make a habit of sleeping around was thinking she wouldn't mind letting him get her out of her dress. She wondered if he'd feel the same way when he saw where she lived, when he had to park his fancy car in the parking lot next to the old motel across from her apartment complex.

No, she reprimanded herself—EJ wasn't like that. He might be wealthy, but he wasn't a snob. He was spiritual, sensual and kind—he wouldn't care about things like that.

Would he? Some rich guys liked to visit the low-end side of town and experience things on the other side of the tracks. Was she being naive?

She shook her head, trying to will away the doubt-

ful thoughts. They emerged out of the well of inse-
curities she still dealt with when confronted with
stressful situations, but she knew better, and closed
her eyes, concentrating on the positive. She didn't
want to let anything ruin this evening. Looking out
the window, she mentally counted the mile markers
as they passed, lulling herself back into a comfortable frame of mind. She didn't realize she'd been
counting aloud.

"Are you feeling okay? Is everything all right?"

She snapped around to face him, realizing EJ must
have been observing her silent struggle with herself,
and smiled wanly.

"I'm fine, sorry. Just internal conversations that
sometimes, well…"

"Show up on the outside?"

"Yeah."

"I know what you mean—when my sister gets
really stressed, or is under a lot of pressure, she talks
to herself in this kind of high-speed mumble that she
doesn't even realize she's doing. She calls it 'leak-
ing.' Like a pressure cooker letting off steam." He
grinned, keeping his eyes on the road.

"That's a really good description. It does feel
like that."

"It sounded like you were counting?"

"Yeah, I do that sometimes." She didn't really
want to get into her little habit, and she hoped he
picked up on the vibe.

"So here we are, after a lovely meal and good company—speaking for myself, anyway." He flashed a charming smile and then continued. "And why would you be feeling stressed?"

She shrugged, and fiddled with some of the lace on the dress, but stopped before she pulled a thread, keeping in mind she had to return it to the shop in the morning. Suddenly she felt like she was in danger of turning into a pumpkin.

"I'm just not used to this."

"To what?"

"You know. This. Fancy dresses, fancy restaurants." She heaved a heavy breath, and laughed lightly. "Fancy dates."

She barely noticed when he pulled into a parking lot that definitely wasn't her apartment. In fact, she realized after a moment that they were down by the Elizabeth River, by the naval shipyards in Portsmouth. She looked around, her voice tentative.

"Where are we?"

"I want to show you something."

He drove through narrow lanes, easily passing through the few checkpoints where the uniformed men at the window seemed to know him, but checked his ID anyway before waving him through. Charlotte didn't feel so much fearful as confused. Those emotions turned into sheer awe as he maneuvered down through narrow roads and alleys, pulling up near two piers that ran along the side of a huge ship.

She had to scrunch down and look up through the window to see the top of it.

"Wow," she whispered.

"She's one of ours."

Charlotte looked at him quizzically in the small confines of the car, and he elaborated with a proud smile.

"We built that. My father's company."

"Really? That's incredible. I'd never seen a real Navy ship before I lived here. I watch them go in and out of the Bay, but I never really caught which one is which. It's smaller than the *Wisconsin*, the one down on the waterfront—what kind is this?"

"The *Wisconsin* is a battleship. This is a destroyer, Burke class. It's smaller, but faster, and generally is used for submarine warfare and battleship defense. Come out and get a better look."

They got out of the car, and the cool breeze off the water chilled her skin, but she barely noticed, she was so busy studying the ship.

"It's so intimidating. Powerful. I always wondered why everyone refers to ships as feminine when they are so obviously male. I mean, really, look at all the parts poking out—it's almost embarrassingly phallic."

EJ laughed, delighted by the observation, and tried to elaborate.

"There are a lot of ideas why ships are referred to as female. Some say it's because they're temperamental and not every man can handle one right," he teased, grinning when she turned her head and gazed at him through narrowed eyes. "Then there is the more logical view that in the Romance languages, the word for ship is always in the feminine. As such, Mediterranean sailors always referred to their ship as she. It just became habit after that. And then there's the idea that early seafarers spoke of their ships in the feminine gender for the close dependence they had on their ships for life and sustenance, like the women who cared for them back home."

Charlotte smiled. "I like the last one."

"I thought so. But I have another idea of my own."

He moved in closer, trapping her body with his, sliding his hands around her middle and she could feel the heat emanating from him.

"What's that?" She shivered, but not from the cold. He moved his fingers lightly along her rib cage, and even though it was through the material of her gown, the touch scorched her.

"I always think of ships and women having beautiful curves. These big ships have been loaded all to hell on the outside, but if you see them as they're being built, you can still see the grace in them, the delicate lines—" he lifted one hand and traced his forefingers along her jaw "—the strong spine…" His hand slipped around back and drew a line from her neck to her backside, where he gently cupped a hand over the curve of her hip as he lowered his lips to hers. She sighed against him, sinking into the kiss, completely seduced.

EJ didn't know why he'd brought her here. He'd never had the urge to show any other woman the ships they built, or anything else so personal. When they'd left the restaurant, he'd intended on just bringing her home and wheedling a way to get into her apartment to see what he could see. But in the battle of cop versus man, man was happily winning as he explored her mouth slowly, taking what she offered as she shuffled a little closer and planted her hands on his shoulders to hold on as the kiss intensified. God, she was sweet.

He was sure he was under some kind of spell, unable to think clearly when she was around, unable to resist being close to her. Working on this case when he was so sexually charged was like going to the grocery store hungry, never a good idea. And he was starving, though food was the furthest thing from his mind. His body quaked, hardening against her. He could barely restrain the urge to take her hard and fast, regardless of where they were, or who might come along.

But he kept the hunger somewhat leashed, and as she moaned against his mouth he slid a hand between them to caress her full breast through the silk, groaning back in appreciation as he felt her nipple harden against his palm. He found the nub through the material and pinched lightly, then again, and Charlotte kissed him more voraciously, begging with her luscious body for more.

He was happy to oblige, touching her everywhere as their mouths refused to part, tongues tangling as they ate each other's kisses and let hands roam everywhere. When she threaded her hands up into his hair and gently pulled his head down a little closer to hers, she leaned in and whispered in his ear, and he felt his cock throb with urgency as her naughty words registered in his brain. Her sultry demands muted the objections, the reminders that he should stop. His body was on overload, and she was too much temptation. He wanted her too much, and the consequences be damned.

Slipping his arm around her and casting a look from side to side to make sure they were alone, he walked with her toward the car, backing up against it, capturing her chin in his fingers, tilting her face toward his.

"Tell me again. Tell me what you want."

His demand was harsh, but she just smiled softly, her cheeks flushed, her breathing quick and light as she held his gaze, but her voice was sure and steady. And sexy as hell.

"I want to get in the back of this gorgeous car and push this dress up so I can feel your hands on me everywhere…and not just through the material."

EJ's breath hitched and his heart pounded as he buried his face in her neck. "More…"

She cried out in desire when he nipped her, and continued, her voice a mere whisper, but the words roared through him.

"I want to stroke your cock and feel it against my skin. I can feel how hard you are, but I want to make you even harder. I want to taste you and bring you to the edge, and then I want to sink down on top of you, taking you inside so deeply you are buried to the hilt, riding you until I come with your tongue in my mouth, so I can scream my pleasure into your soul and feel you come deep inside of me…"

For a woman who said she wasn't very sexually experienced, she sure talked a good game. Growling, EJ pulled her to him roughly, opening the door and thanking the fates he had darkened windows. No sooner were they inside than he was obeying her commands, desperately pushing the silk and lace up as far as he could and letting her pull it the rest of the way over her head.

She was naked except for a small swatch of black silk over her pelvis, and he slipped his hand underneath the material and pulled, glorying in the tearing sound, bending down as well as he could in the confines of the car and trailing kisses up her smooth thighs and over her stomach, touching her everywhere he could reach.

"EJ, I'm so wet already…so hot for you…it's been so long…I need you to make me come."

Her frank talk drove him on in a frenzy and he slid his fingers between her legs, finding out she told the truth. She was hot and slick, so much so he groaned, feeling a little light-headed as he pushed her legs apart and dipped in for a taste.

She writhed beneath him, and he didn't really think about it, sacrificing technique to desperation, tonguing her relentlessly until she bucked beneath him, her hands digging into his hair. Her desperation fueled his, and he couldn't wait anymore, loosening his belt and shoving his pants down, releasing himself, lifting over her, staring down into her passion-soaked eyes. She was still gasping from her orgasm, but managed to remember what he'd forgotten entirely for the first time ever in his life.

"EJ…protection?"

Damn—how could he have forgotten that? Lunging forward over the seat, he opened the glove compartment and felt around in the dark for the small packages he knew he had stashed there. Not that he made a habit of having sex in his car—in fact, it had been near fifteen years since he'd been in this particular situation—but he wasn't worrying about it now. Not when he had this amazing woman hot, ready and naked, sprawled over his backseat.

As he ripped the package, she sat up, taking it from his slightly trembling fingers. He almost objected, but she planted a hand on his chest, and pushed him back into the deep, soft seat.

"Let me."

She obviously wasn't an expert, which he was glad to see as she placed the condom over him carefully with two hands—but not before she dipped her head down and sucked the head of his erection softly until he ground out a plea for her to stop. He was riding on a fine edge of wanting her. One more of her kisses would end it for both of them.

Understanding, she sheathed him a little clumsily and then rose up and over, sinking down over him slowly, accommodating his length in stages, causing him to clench his fists to control himself; she was so tight he almost burst. But even though he was hungry for release, he was more hungry for her, watching her pleasure, and he didn't want it to end too soon.

"Oh, Charlotte, you are incredible. You are so hot…so damned tight…"

She chuckled softly and leaned forward to suck his lower lip as he filled his hands with her breasts, moaning as she started to glide over him, taking him fully in one long stroke, then withdrawing again until he wanted to scream for her to return.

She buried her face in his neck, making the softest, sexiest noises he'd ever heard a woman make, and he moved his hands down to sink his fingers into the generous flesh of her ass, moving her faster over him, controlling the action until his release couldn't be held back and he yelled out his pleasure, lifting up and burying himself deeper as he let go and rode it out, barely aware of her own cries of pleasure, the clenching of her inner muscles milking him until he was limp all over, unable to talk, just letting the pleasure reverberate through his body.

They clung together, melded by sweat and

sticky sex, unable to separate as they rested. EJ broke the silence.

"That was incredible. You are incredible. But I do wish I'd gotten you home first—I feel like a horny teenager doing it in the backseat."

Charlotte pulled back, the ribbon gone from her hair, which flowed wildly around her flushed face, her chocolate-brown eyes shining, pink lips bruised to fuchsia from his kisses.

"I've never been made love to by a handsome man in the backseat of a beautiful car, so I'm not complaining."

He pulled her head down, kissed her, feeling doubts starting to crowd forward and pushed them back away.

"You said it had been a long time for you—do you mind if I ask how long?"

Her brow furrowed, but he realized she was just thinking about his question.

"Seven years."

EJ froze. Seven years? Charlotte had been without sex for seven years?

"Why so long?" He managed the question just before his silence turned awkward. She fell back on her calves, still straddled over him, obviously not in the least bit self-conscious.

"The last time was back in New Hampshire. There was a guy who was helping me with my search. I was depressed one night, he was there. It wasn't a good decision. I was never cut out for meaningless sex."

EJ quirked an eyebrow, taking in the lushness of her breasts, the softness of her skin. As far as he could tell, she was built entirely for all kinds of sex. But then her eyes widened and she covered her mouth with her hand.

"Oh, I'm sorry! I…oh, shoot. I mean, I know this was just sex, and I'm not crazy, you know, like going to go all *Fatal Attraction* on you if this doesn't turn into more, but this wasn't meaningless. Not really. This has been one of the best nights of my life, and I wanted to share this with you even if…you know, we don't see each other anymore."

EJ watched the rush of emotions race across her face and smiled.

"It wasn't meaningless, Charlotte. I don't know what it will mean, but for the moment, it means a lot to me. You're…different."

As he said the words, he realized it was true. His dick was already ready for another go, semihard and nudging at her thigh. He was wondering how this was going to play out—all of the possibilities not very good—when she reached down to remove the rubber and started stroking him again until he was fully erect and breathing hard.

The notion of consequences faded into the darkness as he lifted his hand, tweaking her nipple and watching it bud as she continued to stroke him. He reached down between her legs to return the favor.

He was more relaxed this time, watching her

accept his touch, her eyes glued to his, her bottom lip caught in her teeth as she increased the speed of her movements and started to rock against his hand, sighing.

"Don't close your eyes when you come, Charlotte. I want to see."

She nodded, her breath coming faster. "You, too…"

He reached forward, sliding a finger inside of her, then two, and moving them in conjunction with his knuckles against her clit and her hand moved faster on him, in time with her own excitement. Her breasts were close to his face, swaying softly, and he captured one in his mouth, sending her over the edge. He followed almost directly after, sucking her hard as he came, pumping his fingers into her until they collapsed again.

She laughed breathlessly against his chest, and he didn't know why, but he joined her. As they pulled apart and searched for their clothes, his mind was a scramble. What the hell had he done? What was he going to do now? And most of all, how thankful he was for this night, regardless of what might be on the horizon.

CHARLOTTE WAS QUIET in the passenger seat as EJ sped back along the highway, quieter now due to the late hour, each of them wrapped in their own thoughts after the passionate interlude in the backseat.

What happened now? What would he think when he took her home and found she wasn't really a designer lace and fancy restaurant kind of girl—would she still be as sexy to him?

There was a squeezing sensation in her chest so she took a deep breath, and tried to relax. What had just happened between them had been meaningful, but she feared it may have been more meaningful for her than it was for him. While she hadn't met anyone she could fall for in years, she knew she'd fallen for EJ almost before she met him.

She didn't want to be unreasonable. They'd just met, had one date, made love one time. Well, okay, two times. That was surprising enough; never had she been so carried away with a man, and regardless of what happened she was glad to have experienced that kind of passion at least this once. When she was old and gray, she would still remember.

They took the left onto the long avenue where her apartment was. The moment of truth.

"It's up there, on the right, beach side."

He turned into the parking lot she indicated, and she watched him furtively, checking his reaction, but he simply parked the car, smiled at her and got out. She reached for the handle, only to find he was already opening her door.

She leaned up to kiss him, smiling. "Thanks for a magical night." She turned away, not expecting anything more. Unsure what to expect.

"Charlotte."

She stopped, turned. "Hmmm?"

"Let me see you inside. It's late."

"My apartment is right up there. I'm fine, thanks."

But then he was at her side, his hand on her elbow and she sighed. Time to face the facts; EJ was not about to leave her at the driveway, so she just had to bite it and let him walk her to her door.

"I want to see you again."

If he hadn't held her elbow, she would have tripped.

"You do?"

He stopped, turning her to face him for a moment in the passageway. "Yes, I do. I'm not just going to drop you at your door and walk away."

"Oh. Okay."

"Did you really expect that?"

She shrugged, wrapping her arms around. "I didn't really expect anything. Tonight was wonderful. If nothing else ever came of it, I would always treasure it."

Though her pulse leapt at the thought that he wanted more. Oh, so did she. So much more. She was just afraid to hope.

"You're chilled. Let's get inside."

"My apartment is the last one at the end."

"You have a beach view?"

"Yes, it's one of my very favorite things about living here."

"I used to come down here all the time as a kid. It's a great stretch. A miracle it's remained relatively undeveloped."

"Well, I hope it stays that way."

Charlotte sought her keys in her bag, relaxed by the more normal conversation—EJ didn't seem in the least concerned about where she lived, which went to show that all wealthy people were not necessarily shallow and materialistic.

She stuck her key in the door, but made a soft "oh" sound of surprise when the door pushed open before she even had the key all the way in the lock.

She stopped. Had she left the door open? Had Ronny stopped by and forgotten to lock it? Unlikely; he was always telling her to remember to keep things locked.

"Charlotte. Wait here."

"I'm sure it's just…"

EJ pushed her gently back and gave her a stern look that was all business.

"You just stay put. I mean it."

He pushed the door open a bit more and hugged the wall, entering her apartment. She watched how he moved—stealthily and slowly, like a cat—like someone who was used to moving that way. Curiosity almost trumped her fear, though she jumped a few seconds later when he appeared in the doorway again, his expression tense and concerned.

"EJ?"

"You had better stay out until we can call the police. We don't want to disturb anything."

"What do you mean? What happened?" Panic

made her voice high and sharp, and she pushed past him, unwilling to stay out of her own home. She wanted to know—oh my goodness.

She stood in the doorway, a lump heavy in her throat as her eyes drifted over her cozy little apartment where everything had its place. No more.

Everything had been trashed. Pictures were even pulled from the walls, carpets lifted, drawers emptied. Even her refrigerator had been raided; emptied containers and broken eggs dirtied the kitchen. She started to shake, and sagged against EJ when she felt his solid presence behind her.

"Who would do such a thing? I don't have anything to steal. Oh, no!" She wrenched away from EJ, running to her bedroom. EJ followed closely behind.

"Charlotte, stop. Tell me. What?"

"My laptop! They took my laptop!"

EJ halted in the doorway, looking around her tiny bedroom that was probably once light and cheerfully decorated, but was now just as trashed as the rest of the apartment. Whoever had been here had been looking for something, and they wanted it bad.

"What was on your laptop that someone would want to steal, Charlotte?" Account numbers? Customer information? Evidence? The damning thoughts popped up in his head one after the other. She looked at him in shock and confusion.

"What do you mean? There was nothing of value on my laptop—not to anyone else—but all of my tarot records, my personal files…who would want it? It was an old model, used."

She sat on her bed, looking at him with a blank, wounded stare, and his gut wrenched.

"Charlotte, if you are involved in anything dangerous, if you know any dangerous people who might do something like this, you should tell me now. This is the time to come clean."

She shook her head, her brow furrowing in confusion. "What are you talking about? Come clean about what? I don't know any dangerous people! I don't know why anyone would want to do this to…"

Her voice faded off, as if something occurred to her, and EJ honed in.

"What? What is it? Did you think of something?"

Tears filled her eyes, and he had to hold himself back from going to her. Not now. Not yet.

"My brother, Ronny. Sometimes he hangs with a rough crowd. Maybe…that's all I can think of. Maybe he owed them money, or something—"

"Is Ronny involved in anything illegal?"

"Not that I know of, I mean, he smokes some pot, but that's about it. But his friends are, you know, a little sketchy."

"And he's brought them here?" The thought that Charlotte could be innocent and that her brother could have put her in the path of danger angered EJ, but he choked it back when he saw Charlotte's eyes widen as she watched him. She was already in enough shock.

"Sometimes. He would never let anyone hurt me, though, I know him better than that. He has his problems, but he loves me. He's really very…sweet."

Tears started pouring out, her shoulders shaking as she still sat there in her beautiful dress, her hair still a mess from his hands. He relented against his professional judgment and crossed the room, sitting on the bed and pulling her up against him. Regardless of her level of involvement, she was a victim at the moment, and she was a woman he'd been intimate with. And she was hurting.

"Shhh. Deep breaths. We'll figure it out. We have to call the police."

"I have to find Ronny. I have to make sure he's okay."

"Give me his address. We'll send a unit there right away."

She looked at him, blinking back tears. "You're talking like a cop."

EJ sighed heavily, closing his eyes, and then met her gaze frankly though not without regret. "I am a cop."

6

CHARLOTTE LOOKED AROUND THE tattered surroundings of her bedroom, and then stared down, her fingers having found three frayed pieces of lace hanging from the dress.

"Oh, no!"

EJ leaned in cautiously. "What?"

"The dress. It's not mine! I have to return it in the morning, but look, I must have caught it on something and it's torn!"

"Why do you have to return the dress?"

"The woman at the thrift shop loaned it to me, and I'm supposed to bring it back in the morning. There's no way I could afford something like this, even secondhand, but I wanted something special…"

She couldn't deal with one more thing, and had chosen to not even process what EJ had said to her just moments ago, instead obsessing on the dress. Everything around her was being ripped apart, and she needed to figure out how to fix it.

"Charlotte, look at me. C'mon, darlin'."

He tipped her chin up, bringing her face close to his. She stared into his concerned green eyes.

"You lied to me."

The concern she saw flickered with hints of something else—regret maybe? Guilt?

"Yes. I didn't mean for things to go that way, what happened between us. I shouldn't have let that happen."

"Why not?"

Secrets turned his eyes a deeper shade of moss, she observed.

"Like I said, I'm a police detective. I've been investigating you."

"Me? Why?"

"Your tarot business. The fact that it's a front for online thefts. The more you can tell me about it now, before we have to deal with this, the better. You're obviously not in this alone." He softened his tone, touched her hair. "I want to help, Charlotte, if I can."

She drew away from his touch, her eyes meeting his steadily, and not liking the doubt she read there.

"While I appreciate you wanting to help me, I don't need any help. Not like that. I am not a front for anything. I can't tell you anything, because I am not involved in thefts or anything else! I don't know why you would think I am."

She stood from the bed, walked to a bookcase and began mentally counting the books strewn across the rug, wondering if anything besides her laptop was missing, too distressed to deal with what was happening between them at the moment.

"Charlotte, listen…"

She whirled on him, stopping him in his tracks.

"No, *you* listen. I don't know what's happening here. My home has been violated, my trust has been violated, and I am not going to sit down and take this. I am *not* part of any scam, or any thefts, and I don't know why any of this is happening. Whatever you know, I would appreciate it if *you* would tell *me* right now."

She crossed her arms over her heaving chest, stubbornly refusing to avert her eyes from his, and waited. He nodded, his mouth flattening into a serious, businesslike line, and he did tell her. Who he was, why he was watching her, and what he thought she was guilty of. By the time he was finished, she was numb with rage and confusion.

"I don't understand—just because I did a reading for all of the people who were robbed, you thought it was me doing it? That seems pretty flimsy."

"It is. That's why I was, uh, investigating further. We needed more evidence. But you were our only lead."

"I didn't do it, EJ."

He stared at her hard for several seconds. "Okay. But something has obviously gone bad here, and we have to figure out what it is."

"It could have just been a random break-in."

"Could be. But if it was random, just thieves

looking for stuff to sell, why didn't they take your television or your camera? Yet they only took your computer. And this—" he gestured to the destroyed room "—looks intentional. They weren't just looking for *anything*—they were looking for *something*."

The words chilled her and she started to pace, then stopped abruptly. *Ronny*. Ronny always wanted to borrow her computer, and her computer was missing. She never checked to see what he was up to— could he possibly have been involved in scamming her clients and she had no idea?

Her heart broke at the thought, and then froze—if Ronny was involved, he could be in danger, too. She turned to EJ, grabbing the lapels of his jacket urgently.

"We have to find Ronny. He could be in danger."

"I'll send a car to his address," EJ said, immediately understanding why.

But Charlotte was already out the door before he could dial the first number. "I'm not waiting around for the police. I have to go make sure he's okay."

"Charlotte, wait—you don't know what kind of danger he could be in."

"We have to find out."

EJ DIDN'T LIKE IT one bit that they were on their way to Ronny's apartment—Charlotte had been through enough for one night—but at least she hadn't objected when he'd called for backup and sent someone back to her place. It was going to be a long night.

When he set down his cell phone, she was looking at him quietly, like he was someone she had never met before. He guessed that was more or less the case.

"I'm sorry I lied to you Charlotte. I'm sorry for taking advantage."

"Is that what it was?"

EJ honestly didn't know. Maybe making love to her wasn't so much taking advantage as it was giving in to the buried desires being with her had stirred up, but the results were the same. Maybe the wild way he'd lived his life for the past two years had finally caught up with him, and he'd been a little too casual where he should have been in control.

"I didn't mean to hurt you, regardless of how it might seem."

Amazingly, she reached across the car, and laid her hand on his arm. "I know that, EJ. And I realize that you had a job to do, I really do."

"So you're okay with this?" He found it hard to believe she could just let go of the fact that he'd not only gotten to know her, but had sex with her, under false pretenses. But her next words clearly showed her priorities were elsewhere; he obviously had to get over himself a little, he thought with a self-deprecating sigh.

"Now we just have to figure out what's going on, if anything, and help Ronny."

"If he's the one orchestrating this, Charlotte, I

have to bring him in. He's guilty of serious crimes. And he may try to implicate you—he already has."

She withdrew her hand and wrapped her arms around herself again, not responding. EJ let her be; he wasn't sure how to navigate this mess, but first things first, which meant tracking down Charlotte's brother.

Though his cop's mind reflexively generated a hundred schemes within which Charlotte could still be guilty, he didn't believe them. His gut had been telling him she wasn't a criminal all along, but his mind had refused to listen. But she was going to end up an injured party in this, regardless.

He kicked himself for not checking out Ronny before now. It was such an obvious miss. It also made more sense—the more he learned about Charlotte, the more unlikely it seemed that she was a con artist. He hadn't known her long, but he knew how much her brother—her only family—meant to her. And it would be EJ's job to put him away, if Ronny was involved and if whoever had wrecked Charlotte's home hadn't gotten to Ronny already.

He pulled up in front of the house with the address Charlotte had given him and held to one final, doubting thought: he hoped it wasn't a setup.

He looked at Charlotte, trying to distinguish any telltale clues, but her eyes were glued to the house, fretful and anxious, her hand on the door handle, ready to bolt.

"Wait. Let me talk to the officers first."

Uniformed officers met him at the car, and he spoke to them in low tones, giving them instructions that Charlotte couldn't quite hear, EJ's iron-clad grip on her hand keeping her from rushing into the house.

"Charlotte, I want you to stay here. Let us check it out first. Please."

Though she wanted to object, she knew there could be real danger here and agreed to stay back, if reluctantly. She squeezed EJ's hand.

"Be careful."

His eyebrows lifted in mild surprise and then he turned, walking to the front of the house with the officers, who peered in windows and tried to see anything out of the usual before entering. Within seconds Charlotte could see them hesitate at the door, which pushed open easily, just as hers had.

She held her breath, knowing it wasn't a good sign.

There was no noise, no movement, and she actually jumped when she saw a light flash on inside the apartment.

What was happening? Her mind raced to all the awful things that could have happened, and she took a step forward, only to stop when EJ showed up on the porch. He signaled to her to come in.

But before she could so much as take a step forward, a car peeled around the corner and barreled down the street. Charlotte stood, looking at the vehicle in blank confusion, the sound and speed startling her.

She was still frozen on the sidewalk as EJ yelled

and ran down the steps, lunging in her direction. The officers appeared on the porch, and Charlotte hit the ground very hard, broken glass shattering somewhere and sounds of men shouting and muffled gunfire filling the air.

Her arm hurt but she didn't move, hearing EJ's harsh breathing and muffled curses as the car sped away. When she felt the weight of his body lift from hers, she still didn't move, unsure what was going on or what she was expected to do.

"Charlotte, get in the car and stay down."

EJ had opened the car door and practically threw her in the backseat, pushing her down into the leather. She thought she heard him whisper, "Sorry, sweetheart" as he closed the door and rushed back toward the house. As the numbness of surprise passed, she swallowed her breath in gulps and lifted up, just enough to peer through the backseat window. EJ was on the sidewalk in front of the steps; he and one of the other officers were crouching over something—someone—the other officer.

"Oh, my God," Charlotte whispered, reaching for the handle. Someone had been hurt. She opened the door and ran up to them, clamping her hand over her mouth as tears burnt her eyes when she saw the dark stain on the cement sidewalk surrounding the officer.

"Is he…?"

EJ looked up, bleak. "Charlotte, get back in the car. They could come back."

"Is he dead?"

"No. But it's bad. Help's on the way, please get back in the car."

"I want to help."

"There's nothing you can do, darlin'."

Sirens screamed in the distance, and Charlotte took a few steps backward, though she didn't obey EJ's orders—how could she? How could she just go cower in fear as this man lay dying out in the open on the sidewalk? She stepped forward, crouching, and took the wounded officer's limp hand in hers, willing him her energy to hold on.

"Charlotte," EJ bit out her name, but then looked deeply into her eyes, his own gaze weary and sad. He signed deeply, relenting. "Okay."

Charlotte flinched when tires screeched to the curb, but she knew this time it was the ambulance and more police. As EMTs rushed up the sidewalk, shouting to make room, she let go of the officer's hand and backed away. Chaos ensued, and she felt as if she were in a fog, drifting up the steps and into the house, away from the horrible intensity of the moment. That man had to live. She couldn't bear the thought that someone died because of something Ronny might have gotten involved in.

She pushed a battered, plastic shade away from the window—she'd always offered to make Ronny some curtains, but he thought they were girly—and looked on as the officer was carted into the ambulance. EJ stood on the sidewalk talking with another man and a tall, gorgeous woman who looked really pissed off.

Were they all cops? Suddenly she felt very alone, and very scared. Ronny was gone, her home was devastated, she was suspected of being a criminal, someone had been shooting guns over her head, and EJ was certainly not who she thought he was—what was going to happen to her next?

Looking down, she noticed she had some blood-stains on the hem of the dress, and felt her stomach clench. The scrap of material she wore was unimportant, relatively speaking, but she'd made a promise to Phoebe, and now the dress was ruined. It was the last straw. With a peek back out the window, she headed for the back door.

"DID YOU FIND ANYTHING inside the house?"

EJ had called Ian to the scene as soon as he'd called for an ambulance, and he shook his head.

"Not yet. We didn't really have time. I came back out to get Charlotte, and then all hell broke loose."

"Any idea who was in the car?"

"Hell, no."

"Will she know?" Ian tipped his head toward Charlotte, who was peeking out through a shade. EJ knew he was walking a thin line on this one—to say his behavior was unprofessional didn't even begin to describe it. Ian would want to take Charlotte in for questioning, but EJ had a gut feeling that wouldn't get them anywhere.

"I don't think so. She seems pretty clueless about the entire thing."

Sarah stepped forward. "Are you making that assessment with your big head or your little one?"

EJ's temper flared, his emotions stripped too thin to put up with Sarah's shit tonight, and he stepped forward, toe-to-toe with his colleague. "Don't push it, Jessup."

Ian sighed. "Though badly phrased, I think it's a fair question, EJ. Not that I don't normally trust your instincts, but it could have been you getting loaded into that ambulance tonight. If you're off on this one, for whatever reason, you need to be straight about it."

EJ took a deep breath, neither he nor Sarah breaking their standoff, and he answered Ian. "I've seen her house, spent time with her, asked her straight on about what's going on—she could be lying, I've played out the scenarios, but I don't think so. There's a better chance her brother's been using her to run his own scams. He sounds like trouble waiting to happen, and probably got in over his head." He took a step back, watching as Charlotte stepped back from the window. "She didn't stay down. When Nate went down, she came and sat with him. Held his damned hand."

"That's hardly—" Sarah's comment was cut short by a look from Ian.

"Okay. They're at her place now, brushing for prints, and we'll do the same here, though it doesn't look like anyone was here. We'll go with your gut for now. Though whatever she's involved in, it's gone way beyond theft," Ian concluded.

"Agreed." EJ paused for a moment, then added, "How'd they know we were here?"

"Huh?" Ian said.

"The shooters. How'd they know where we were?"

"A bug maybe. A neighborhood snitch. Could be anything," Ian said, shrugging.

"Could be a leak," EJ said, blowing out a breath.

Ian's eyes widened. "You think someone at the station told them you were here?"

"I called in for backup, for someone to come to the house, then this happens. It's not impossible."

"Shit," Ian said.

"Yeah."

"That would put a whole new spin on things—who could have their hands in something that reached that far?" Ian asked.

The question settled between them, and EJ rubbed his hands over his face, shaking his head.

"I have to get in there. See how's she's doing." He looked Ian in the eye. "You know I can't bring her in if there's a chance someone on the inside set this up."

"So what are you going to do?" Ian asked.

"I don't know, but I'll be in touch."

"This won't go down well. She's involved, even if she's not guilty—with one of our men down, there isn't going to be much patience waiting for her to tell what she knows, even if it's not much. They'll want to know why she hasn't been brought in."

"Tell them I'm on it." EJ met Ian's doubtful glance solidly before turning and walking back into the house.

CHARLOTTE QUICKLY WENT to Ronny's bedroom, looking for something less obvious to wear, and found his clothes thrown around, and his one beat-up suitcase gone. He'd taken off, apparently. The thought provided her some small bit of relief—she'd been afraid he might have met with a much worse fate. A piece of white paper was on the bed, and she moved toward it, slowly, and then read the brief message scrawled out in Ronny's rough handwriting.

> Charlotte, so sorry, hon, I was doing this for us. For you. But there could be some big trouble, so watch yourself. I'll try to straighten it out, but won't be in touch for a while. Love, Ronny

Charlotte stared at the note, her voice thin.

"Oh, Ronny, what have you done?"

She grabbed the note as she heard the screen door in the front hallway squeak open and shut. EJ. She had no time to find clothes, she had to go. She had to find her brother before he did another stupid thing.

Quickly, she pushed up the window by the head-board of the bed and swung her legs over the sill, unconcerned at this point what further damage happened to the dress. She was done in on that score anyway. Kicking her shoes off, she slid to the damp ground, heard EJ calling her name somewhere inside the apartment, and took off at a run.

She knew the backlots well enough to find her way to the next neighborhood, and looked around frantically for a taxi. She couldn't trust EJ—he had a job to do, but that job meant she could be spending the rest of the night in a police station ratting out her brother instead of looking for him, and she wanted to find him before the cops did. Or before whatever nasty people who were after them did.

Luck was on her side. She didn't see EJ behind her, and a taxi pulled up at the curb. She got in, but wasn't sure where to tell the driver to go. It hit her then: Rascal's. It was a dive on the edge of town where Ronny and his friends hung out. She'd only been there once or twice, and she didn't really know anyone, and doubted they'd remember her. But they might know where Ronny is.

She directed the driver, and sat back, chewing on her thumb as they drove to the outer edges of the city, where there were fewer people and darker streets, but she barely noticed. Spotting a twenty-four-hour convenience store, she asked the driver to stop and ran in, purchasing a pair of cheap scissors before moving on.

While she thought about her plan, and how she might contact Ronny, she ruthlessly cut the French lace she wore off at the knee, going as evenly as she could so she'd look a little more casual and avoid drawing any attention to the bloodstain on the hem. Smoothing her hair, she handed the driver her credit card and hoped she had enough money on it to pay for the fare, and exhaled in relief when he handed it back to her without a problem.

The cab drove away, leaving her standing in the dusty parking lot with the sounds of tree frogs and other night creatures humming behind her and the booming sound of rock music and raucous laughter thrumming from the bar.

Straightening her back, she took a deep breath and headed for the door. She wasn't in any danger. It was just a bar, which meant there were waitstaff, bartenders and cooks—no one was going to hurt her here. The most she might have to endure would be some comments or leers, and she could deal with that.

EJ RACED BACK OUT to the sidewalk, looking around sharply, and didn't see a thing. Sarah was gone, and Ian was on his cell phone in the front seat of his car. EJ slid in beside him, covering his mouth with his palm for a second, and then looked at Ian, who clicked off his phone and met EJ's glance.

"I lost her."

"What? How could you lose her? She was right there in the window."

"She must have bolted through the back when I came in, or while we were dotting the I's and crossing the T's out here." He slammed the heel of his hand into the dash. "Shit. I can't believe we let this happen."

"Want to put out an APB?"

EJ considered. "No. It's still possible whoever's after her and her brother could be clued into the police communications. She's in enough danger already. At least if we don't know where she is, maybe no one else does, either."

"True. But to disappear that quickly she had to have some help. She caught a bus, took a cab, or hitched, but someone, somewhere, knows where she was going, so it won't be hard to find out. Let's head back to the lab."

"Shouldn't you get home to Sage?"

"She'll call me if something happens."

EJ nodded curtly, pissed at himself, at Charlotte, and hoping desperately that they found her before anyone else did.

"Okay, let's go."

7

"I'VE GOT HER."

Ian slapped the desk, his exclamation pulling EJ away from his own inquiries as Ian slammed down the phone, smiling like the cat who got the cream.

"Well, whether she's guilty or not, she's not very slick. Took General taxi and paid with her credit card about an hour ago. They dropped her at a place called Rascal's. Here's the address. You know it?"

EJ nodded. "I've been past it. A real dive on the outskirts." His gaze darkened as he grabbed his jacket. Thankfully he kept a change of clothes at the office and wouldn't have to go to the roadhouse in his expensive suit. He'd have trouble before he made it through the door that way. But in jeans, sweatshirt and Norfolk Tide baseball cap, he should fit right in. He hoped.

"What the hell did she go there for?" he wondered out loud.

"Either she's meeting up with someone, or she's looking for someone. Or trying to disappear."

"Could be she knows where her brother is after all."

"Want backup?"

EJ shook his head, feeling a lethal mix of emotions that he couldn't quite sort through, but he pushed them down, becoming cool and focused. He shoved his nine-millimeter in his belt under his jacket.

"No. I'll get her."

"It could be she didn't make a mistake. Maybe she wants to be found."

"A trap?"

"Could be. You should have backup."

"No, it'll scare her off. I want to make a quiet approach, see what's going on, not go in there with sirens blaring. And it could be it was a stupid mistake."

"Dangerous assumption."

"I'll take my chances."

"HOOO-DOGGIE! Come over here, sweet thang, and sit on papa's lap for a lil' while."

A chorus of laughter went up as Charlotte made her way through the bar, telling herself the comments were not aimed at her. She kept her eyes on the bar and made her way to it, sitting as quickly as she could and signaling the bartender—she thought she remembered his name was Frank, but she wasn't sure.

The smoke in the place choked her, and she counted the bottles lined up on the back of the bar, striving to look careless and unperturbed as one large, smelly man took the seat next to her. She held her breath again, and closed her eyes in relief when he ignored her and turned to the guy next to him.

She wasn't so lucky the second time. Someone swaggered up, and wasn't about to be ignored, tapping her on the shoulder. She set her jaw and turned, her eyes widening when she took in the very threatening countenance of the man who towered over her as she faced him from her position on the stool. He didn't look like a barfly, and he definitely wasn't anyone she'd seen before. He was…handsome, for one thing. He wasn't smoking, and he smiled, just a little.

"Ms. Gerard?"

He knew her name. She recoiled, looking around her, wondering what was going on. Was he a cop? Or one of the men who wrecked her apartment and shot at her? The man leaned in, planting his hands on the bar on either side of her. His breath was minty, not alcoholic. A bad guy wouldn't have clean breath, would he?

"Ms. Gerard?"

"Yes. How do you know my name?"

"We know someone in common."

She grasped his forearm with her hand, no longer afraid. "Ronny? My brother? Do you know where he is?"

The man's eyes narrowed to slits. "No. Actually, we were looking for you. Your computer didn't offer up the information we needed, so we decided to come directly to the source."

"You! You wrecked my home!"

He slanted a smile. "Not personally, no. Why don't you come with me? I have someone who'd like to talk with you."

She crossed her arms resolutely over her chest. "I'm not going anywhere with you. And I don't believe you—you must know what happened to Ronny."

He removed one hand from the bar to push his jacket back, just far enough to show her he had a gun inside there. She felt light-headed and closed her eyes. What had she gotten herself into? She slid from the stool, the strange man's hand like a vise around her arm, and walked slowly behind him.

In a last-ditch attempt, she mouthed the word *help* to anyone whose eye she could catch, and was gratified to see someone—maybe the man who had cat-called her when she entered the bar—stand up, eye the man ahead of her suspiciously and step forward with a few of his very large friends.

"Hey, mister. Seems like maybe the lady doesn't feel like leaving with you tonight." The big man laughed, looking down at her with a leer. She ground her teeth and smiled at him, unsure whether she was leaping from the pan into the fire, but was willing to take her chances.

The man who held her stopped, took a deep breath and turned, facing the large men with as much of a good ol' boy smile as he could muster.

"Now, sir," he said, dragging Charlotte up hard

against him so she could feel the butt of the gun through his jacket. "This here is my wife, and I'm set to take her home. What would you think if you found your woman, dressed like this, in the middle of the night, in this kind of place? Doesn't a man have a right to come get her?"

The big man pinched his chin and thought. Charlotte started to speak up, but her captor twisted her wrist painfully and her words just came out on a groan. Her plan was failing, she could see by the look in the redneck guy's eyes. This wasn't a liberal guy—he'd surely think a man had a perfect right to drag "his woman" from the bar. No sooner had she thought it and the passel of men backed off, muttering things about not interfering in private matters between a man and a woman.

"Nice try, sweetheart."

The tall man pulled her forward again, and she resisted, but stopped when he shot her a deadly look. They walked through the door, and through the parking lot. She started to shake with fear.

Suddenly the man's grip on her wrist loosened, and he fell backward with a grunt. As her kidnapper crumpled to the dirt, she looked up and stared into cold, angry green eyes.

EJ BENT TO THE GROUND, patting the unconscious man down, taking his gun and his wallet, before returning his attention to Charlotte. Without a word, he took her by the shoulders, pushing her toward his car, and she gasped, moving like a marionette being pushed and dragged from place to place.

But EJ wasn't feeling too gentle at the moment, his anger and the fear he'd felt when he saw her being dragged out into the parking lot consuming him. Whoever the guy was, he was carrying some serious firepower, and EJ didn't want to think of what could have happened to her. He was surprised when she whirled on him.

"Stop pushing me! What right do you have—" He cut her off, slapping his hand over her mouth to quiet her, and actually putting her in the seat of his car, arrest style, hand on head. She glared up at him, rebounding, and he leaned in close.

"Should I cuff you, princess? Because I'm more than willing."

She backed off and settled in with a resentful look, and he went around to his own side, satisfied that she wasn't going to take off on him again. If she did, he'd catch her before she got too far, and this time he would cuff her.

Pulling away from the parking lot in a spray of dust and gravel, they drove down the highway toward the city, silent until he pulled over, comfortable with the distance between them and the roadhouse, unsure of his next move. He knew Ian expected him back, but this wasn't about Ian. What happened next depended on Charlotte.

Putting the car in Park, he turned and pinned Charlotte with his stare, hardening his heart to her desperate eyes, the pulse he saw hammering frantically in her throat.

"You said you weren't guilty of anything, Charlotte—so why did you take off?"

"I knew you were going to bring me in, and that would have been time lost in finding Ronny."

"That bar was one of his hangouts?"

She nodded, looking down at her hands, where her fingers played with the ragged ends of the shortened dressed. Her voice was subdued when she spoke.

"I should have known. I should have seen it, his cards have indicated some trouble, but I never thought of something like this. I could have helped him."

She thought she was responsible for what trouble her brother was in? EJ sat back in disbelief, processing the information, but realizing it was consistent with what he knew about her so far. It sounded like she'd do just about anything for Ronny, including putting herself in the path of danger.

"Who was the guy dragging you out?"

"I don't know. He said we had a mutual friend, and he was bringing me to meet him."

"He has your brother?"

"He said no—they wanted me."

EJ sighed, leaning forward, turning her toward him and planting his large hands on her shoulders, shaking her lightly.

"What's happened to your brother is not your fault, Charlotte. In fact, it's starting to look to me like it could be quite the opposite. I know you think you can see things in the cards, but there's no way you could have seen something like this coming. Ronny is obviously involved with some very dangerous people, and it looks like he's involved you, too."

"You don't understand." She spat the words, pulling away from him, unsure what to think about anything. "He's my brother. I know he's had a hard time. I should have paid more attention, I should have—"

"This has gotten really serious, darlin'. It's bigger than you and your brother. A cop was shot, and the people who are standing at his bedside are going to want to know why. You're the only one who we know is connected right now—" he held his hand up to stem her objection "—I said connected, not guilty. But they'll want someone's head. And I would rather it not be yours."

She blinked, looking at him warily. "You don't think I'm guilty?"

EJ was quiet for several moments, sifting through his confusing thoughts, his anger subsiding. He listened to his gut, which had served him well so far.

"No, I don't think you are guilty. But I think your brother is in this up to his neck, and I'm going to find out why. There are apparently some very bad people after him—why they came out shooting tonight, I have no idea. A message, I guess."

"Or maybe they were trying to keep us from finding something."

"Like what?"

She shrugged, but he realized she could be right. The entire episode could have been a distraction, to keep them out of the house. Perhaps whoever had trashed Charlotte's home hadn't had a chance to look through Ronny's place, and had been trying to keep them out. But by shooting a cop, they had made the house inaccessible to everyone—unless there was a dirty cop on their payroll. Things just weren't adding up.

"We need to go back to the house." Charlotte's voice was resolute.

"No, that's not an option. The cops have been all over it—if there's something to find, they'll find it. I've got to report the incident at the roadhouse, and get this ID to Sarah and Ian. Then we have to find someplace to stay, to lay low until we know something about what's going on."

"Where?"

"I have some ideas."

Without another word, he pulled back out onto the pitch-dark highway, and drove east.

CHARLOTTE WASN'T SURE where she was when she woke up, but it smelled nice. And it was warm. And solid. She snuggled in closer, feeling safe and... Wait.

The feeling of her world being tipped seriously

out of balance returned, and she sat up sharply in the bed, looking around the strange room. Listening to the chirping sounds of creatures outside the screened windows, she could swear she heard ocean surf. It was all peaceful, but unfamiliar.

Then, looking down, she saw the source of the warm comfort she'd awakened to. EJ.

Her hand flew to her chest, only to find it stalled halfway—he'd *cuffed* her, the other link attached to his own wrist. She knew without feeling that she was naked—she wasn't wearing the silky lace gown any longer.

Reflexively, she pulled the sheet up around her with her other hand, and then looked down at the man sleeping beside her; EJ was still fully clothed and sleeping on top of the covers. The events of the previous hours came rushing back, and she sighed, her body sinking back into the lush pillows. She guessed after what had happened between them the previous evening, being naked with the man wasn't a big deal. And she almost couldn't blame him for handcuffing her. Almost.

"Are you okay?" EJ's hushed whisper drifted softly through the darkness, though he hadn't moved a muscle. She turned her head and saw he still lay in the same position with his eyes shut. She wondered if she'd imagined him speaking, but then he turned his head to her, just looking across the pillows in the darkness.

"I'm naked." The bald statement escaped before

she could think, and she looked away. "And I'm in handcuffs."

"I didn't think you'd be comfortable sleeping in the dress. It was getting pretty ratty. And you were completely passed out by the time we got here. But I didn't want to take any chances on you waking up and taking off again."

"I wouldn't have."

"Sure you wouldn't." His voice conveyed his doubt. "But this way I could get some peaceful shut-eye, too."

Not too peaceful, she thought, spotting the shadow of his gun on the nightstand.

"Thanks, I guess. I can't believe I was sleeping so soundly I didn't even realize you'd undressed me." She blew out a breath, looking back in his direction. "Where is 'here'?"

"My sister's summer house. We're about two hours up the shore, in Assateague."

"In Maryland?"

"Yeah. It was the only place I could think of to disappear for a while on short notice."

"I still don't understand why we need to disappear. Did you hear anything about that officer? Is he okay?"

"I checked in a few hours ago, and he was critical but stable. He hasn't regained consciousness yet, but they're hoping for the best."

"Does he have a family?"

"He's not married, but he does have a family. Parents, siblings."

"Who was the man who tried to grab me? Do you know?"

"They're running his license. We'll know soon."

She mumbled something unintelligible, an irrational sense of guilt and sadness clogging her throat, blocking any response. She'd lived through dark times before, but she'd thought all of that was in the past. Now a man had almost died, her brother was missing, her home was destroyed, and she was... what? A suspect? A target?

EJ had said he believed her, that he was protecting her, but how could she know for sure? He obviously didn't trust her, but she supposed she'd brought that on herself. If he hadn't shown up when he did, who knew what could have happened to her if that man had gotten her in his car? She could be dead in a ditch by the side of the road by now, too.

An encroaching feeling of helplessness and desperation surrounded her, she almost forgot EJ's presence, until she felt a rustling of the blankets as his weight shifted on the bed, and the room became bathed in soft light when he clicked on a bedside lamp. She squeezed back tears, gripping the blankets in a painfully tight grasp.

"Charlotte."

She looked at him, swallowing at how handsome he was, tousled by sleep, his clothes completely rumpled, his gaze sleepy but filled with great concern. He held out his hand to her, and she released her grip on the blanket to take it, unsure of what he was offering, but needing the connection. His warm fingers massaged hers, the metal of the cuffs clinking together. His voice was soothing, and his gaze never wandered from her face.

"This is in no way your fault. You have to believe that."

She took a deep breath, and nodded. Deep down, she still felt she should have noticed something, should have had some sense of what was going on with Ronny, but she also acknowledged that her brother was an adult man, and she didn't control his actions.

"I know, I guess, on some level, that that's true. But I can't help but feel…bad."

"I know. You have every right in the world to feel that way." His voice lowered. "C'mere, darlin'. Let me hold on to you for a little while."

Her heart tripped a little faster, and she kept the blanket hitched up as she scooted over closer to him, breathing in the wonderful scent she'd awakened to.

Images of making love with him in the car flashed in front of her eyes. It felt like a dream, like it had happened years ago rather than just hours, but her body dampened in response to the memory and his nearness. It was unusual, but undeniable, that she wanted him so much. So she sat up a little and tucked in underneath the arm he stretched out for her. God, he felt so good. She cuddled her cheek down into the intersection of chest and shoulder, sighing.

"Better?"

She nodded, loving the feel of the hard muscles of his chest underneath of his shirt as she snuggled closer. Her fingers slid in between the buttons, touching his skin, and she thought she heard him catch his breath before he grasped her seeking fingers in his other hand.

"Just rest easy, darlin'. Relax, think good thoughts."

She felt him kiss her hair as he moved her fingers gently back to a less sensuous position and melted under the sweetness of the caress. She sniffled, tears welling up again, but she pushed them back and felt EJ's arms tighten around her, the one solid thing in her world, and she held on tight.

"It's going to work out, Charlotte. Things will be okay."

"It's just gotten so complicated so quickly, I feel like I can hardly keep track of what's going on."

He reached down and tipped her chin up, looking deeply into her eyes. "I'll keep you safe. I promise that."

"It's not me I'm so worried about. Ronny is out there somewhere, involved in God knows what. That poor officer is in the hospital, and Phoebe could lose her job over me. And then there are all the other people I have responsibilities to. I am supposed to be reading cards tomorrow, and walking dogs, and instead here I am, and everything is falling apart."

"Who's Phoebe?"

"Oh, she's the girl at the thrift shop who lent me the dress. She said her boss wouldn't be back for a few days, so no one would know if I got it back there this morning—undamaged, of course. I know I shouldn't have borrowed it. I knew it then, but I wanted to look like the kind of woman you expected me to be."

His eyebrows crunched in the middle, the ends of his gorgeous mouth turning down. "What do you think I expected?"

She sat up a little, the sheet not quite covering the fullness of her cleavage as she did so.

"Someone sophisticated and well put together. Someone who wasn't going to show up at the best restaurant in Norfolk in discount clothing."

To his credit, he looked surprised as she elaborated, and she reached up, touching his face.

"Really, EJ, I've seen who you are, how you live. The kind of family you come from. You are so elegant and refined, so gentlemanly. And I don't even know how to order off a fancy menu. Even though you're a cop, none of that other stuff goes away." She took a deep breath, looking down at her fingers wrapped around the edge of the sheet, before going on.

"Now that you know who I am, and all the trouble that's surrounding me, are you really all that interested in me anymore? I have no family except a brother who's probably a criminal, I live in a cheap little apartment that's been completely ruined, and I wear borrowed clothes and don't have an education or a real job. Not exactly your type."

He pulled back, mild surprise turning to something stronger, and she tugged the sheet up, suddenly uncomfortable.

"EJ?"

He blinked, his voice quiet when he spoke. "I didn't realize I came off as such a snob."

Her hand flew to her mouth, causing her to drop the sheet again, and she shook her head emphatically. "No, I didn't mean that! I just meant…I don't know exactly, but it was more about me than you. Just that I'm not…I'm—"

He leaned in, his eyes intense, and though he didn't touch her, she felt like squirming. "What? What are you, Charlotte? Not good enough for me? So sure that I'm going to turn my back the moment you don't wear designer clothes?"

His lips thinned, and she realized she'd actually hurt him, and was stunned by the fact.

"What a woman wears is not high on my list of necessities, though you did look stunning in that dress. But here's a news flash: you look stunning out of it, too. You're sexy, soft and entirely too concerned about others and not nearly concerned enough about yourself, from what I can tell. And though there have been times when you have been scarily perceptive, especially with those cards of yours, there are other times, like now, when you can't see past your nose."

She felt her eyes widen in response to his words, and gasped when he reached out, tugging her up against him, his jaw set, his eyes moving over her hungrily.

"I've played the part of the gentleman, Charlotte, but that's not all there is to me. Not by far. I have money, and breeding—whatever that all means— but at the moment, it doesn't seem to matter."

Barely able to catch her breath, she couldn't look away from his intense stare. "What do you mean?"

"I can see who *you* are, Charlotte, and it makes me crazy. I want you so much I can barely think straight, and that's not a familiar, or comfortable, place for me to be. Even when I shouldn't have wanted you, when I thought you were a criminal, I couldn't keep my hands off you. Before I met you in person, I knew I wanted you."

He rubbed his thumbs over the bare skin of her arms, his voice becoming raspy with unmasked desire. "I came here tonight with the best of intentions, to protect you, and had every single intention to keep my damn hands off you."

She shuddered as his palms moved over the bare skin of her back, pushing the sheet farther away.

"I told myself you'd been through enough, and I wasn't going to take advantage of a woman in your vulnerable position. But all I know right now is I want you to see *me*. Not a romanticized image of someone you've cooked up in your head, not a cop or anything, but a man. A man who can't keep his hands off you. So right now, I'm not feeling like much of a gentleman."

His hand stole up to her shoulders and pulled her over top of him, the sheet sliding down to her waist, exposing her to his view. He devoured her with a lustful glance, possessing her with his eyes before he matched his mouth to hers.

Charlotte wanted to respond, to tell him she did see him for the man he was, to tell him she didn't just think of him as a shallow romantic prince or her personal protector. But the desperation of his kiss, the need that fueled it, overcame her. She wrapped her arms around his neck, weaving her fingers tightly into his hair and crushing her mouth into his to try to let him know how she was feeling in the only way she could. The muscles of his neck were tense and hard beneath her fingers, and she massaged them with her fingertips as they kissed. She wanted to send a clear message: if he wanted her, she was his.

When he yanked the sheet away completely, she tugged at his shirt, wanting him out of his clothes as quickly as possible. He was obviously in agreement, his breathing labored as he slipped off of the bed, forgetting the cuffs, his linked arm tugging at hers before he got very far.

"I think we can take those off now, don't you?" She looked at him from beneath her lashes, his arousal obvious. He stared at her, as if considering, then, pulled a small drawer out from the bed-stand, and he took out a small key. He loosened his cuff, and she scooted forward, holding out her wrist, but gasped when he took her other hand, pulled it forward, and locked it into the loose cuff.

"EJ! What are you—don't you trust me to stay here with you?"

His grin was wicked, his intentions clear. Charlotte's lips formed a silent "oh" as she watched him undress and understood his restraining her had nothing to do with law enforcement.

"As much as I love those warm, soft hands on me, honey, this time, I want you at my mercy. Do you mind?"

EJ watched her slow smile with primal satisfaction, her eyes caressing his naked body with a sweeping glace.

"Not one bit."

8

EJ WANTED TO POUNCE on her and take her fast, sate the hunger that had spiked in his soul, but he intended to do just the opposite, and enjoy every exquisite second, and take her as slowly as he possibly could. He wanted to expose every secret, know every soft, unexplored place of her body. He wanted her completely.

He moved forward, gently lifting her arms, joined at the wrist by the cuffs, and dragged his tongue down the length of the inside of her arm, from palm to shoulder, before taking her mouth in a carnal kiss. It was as if every woman he'd ever made love to were stops on a long journey to finding this one woman, who aroused him more than any other ever had.

He pushed her back gently, lifted himself up over her and planted his long length firmly between her thighs. He shuddered when his erection graced the silky inside of her leg, and nearly lost it. He was dying to get inside of her, but instead just teased the hungry core of her sex with the tip of his erection, pushing inside slightly, then pulling out to slide along the slick alley between her legs, stimulating her until she was crying out and arching up underneath him.

He backed off, denying his own hunger, his breath coming hot and heavy as he watched her flushed form writhe on the messed bed, the sight of her restrained hands fueling some basic passion within him.

He levered up over her, placing a hand on either side of her breasts and pushing them together, fitting them closely so he could take both peach-colored nipples in his mouth at once and nipped her with gratification when she yelled his name, bucking. He sucked hard, then licked, burying his face in the fragrant fullness of her bosom and found, when he finally moved away, that his own hands were shaking.

"Charlotte, I swear, you are the most delicious woman…I have ever been with. I can't keep my mouth off of you…"

He returned to her skin, burning a path down her belly and beyond, holding her thighs wide apart with his hands while exploring the slick folds of her sex with his mouth, stroking her with his tongue into an orgasm that had her fighting the hold of his hands, tightening her legs around his shoulders and crying out into the room. EJ delved even farther into her, unwilling to stop even though she'd come, moving down her legs and eating every inch of her, committing each spot to memory.

"EJ, please, I want you."

Charlotte felt like a hot-buttered noodle, reveling in the feeling of being totally female and totally ravished. Her mouth was raw from kisses and the scraping of his light beard, the spot between her legs melted and craved more of him.

As he moved up over her, she licked his shoulder, savoring the taste of his skin as he nudged against her again, teasing and torturing. She wanted to touch him, to pull him into her, but her hands were still bound. She had expected frustration at the restraints, but instead she felt stimulated by the denial, open to him and at his bidding. It was completely erotic, and made her skin tingle at every touch.

He lifted up, the separation eliciting a cry of protest from her as she saw him reach for the key again and move to uncuff her. And just when she was totally getting into it.

"I want you free. Free to move when I'm inside you."

Oh, she thought, not missing the handcuffs one little bit, suddenly.

He stood, looking at her with raw desire in his eyes, and she crawled forward on the bed, watching him watch her, his chest heaving, glistening with a fine film of sweat, his hands clenched as his gaze bore into her. She stayed planted on her hands and knees, looking at him seductively, sensing he was holding on to the last bits of his control. And she wanted to shred them.

"Whatever you want, EJ. I won't hold anything back."

He growled and his cock jerked with arousal at her words, and she smiled, wicked and wanton. He walked toward her, his erection tantalizingly even with her mouth for a moment, and she suddenly couldn't resist tasting. He stilled, freezing, as he seemed to intuit her intentions, and edged a little closer, encouraging her.

The heat from his body radiated out like a furnace and she thought she could feel a sizzle as her lips closed over the smooth head of his shaft and slid all the way down in a wet, testing caress. He cursed out loud and wove his hands into her hair, directing her but not forcing her as she experimented to find what pleased him and sighed against his skin when he reached farther down to massage a breast while she sucked him to the edge.

"Charlotte, I need to get inside you. Now."

She pulled back, gasping as he caught her by the waist, swinging her around until her backside faced him and her knees perched precariously on the edge of the bed. But she didn't have to worry about sliding off—EJ was solid and close behind her, massaging her bottom with both hands, spreading her and pushing forward until he was buried deep inside, extracting groans of sheer pleasure from them both.

The soft cotton of the comforter teased her nipples to excruciating sensitivity as he moved behind her, his own animalistic sounds filling the room as their flesh slapped together echoing the rhythm of their urgency.

Charlotte dug her fingers into the blankets, pushing back for all she was worth, grinding against him in the total pursuit of the pleasure that hovered again, just past the horizon.

When he leaned forward, sucking the tender skin in the middle of her back, she lost it, a blinding orgasm hit, the sensation blasting through her, disintegrating every inch of her to her fingertips. Only seconds later she heard his cry of release as he let go, still buried deep, filling her with a different sense of satisfaction.

They stayed linked in their positions for a few minutes, catching their breath, and finally Charlotte moved forward, collapsing on the bed and EJ slid up alongside of her, pulling her into his arms.

"You're amazing, Charlotte." He leaned down, capturing her mouth and kissing her until she couldn't breathe, but they both came up laughing. "I can't seem to stop wanting you. You're like a drug."

"You're not so bad yourself." She laughed, kissing him lightly, then drawing back when she saw his expression fall, his eyes close.

"Damn it."

Charlotte put her hand to his face, concerned.

"What?"

EJ turned his head to press a kiss into her palm,

his gaze regretful, and she felt her heart clench in reaction, stealing her breath as he spoke.

"We didn't use anything."

His eyes bore down into hers, and she didn't quite understand for a second until his meaning dawned on her. They'd forgotten contraception. Tired, emotionally drained, needy and pushed to the edge, precautions had been the last thing on her mind. Or on his, apparently.

"Oh."

She counted mentally. She'd had her last period two weeks before, but she really had no idea if this was a "safe" time or not. She'd never really committed the schedule to memory. Sex had been such a nonfactor in her life that she'd given up the pill years ago, disliking the effects of synthetic hormones and figuring she'd deal with the issue when it arose.

Well, it had just arisen.

And surprisingly, she felt no panic at all. Not even an iota. Maybe her life was in such chaos that she'd developed a resistance to any new shocks, or maybe it was the safety of the night, and being here with EJ. Maybe things would be different in the morning, but right now the slip-up didn't seem to be all that big of a concern to her. However, he still looked really worried. Probably because pregnancy was the least of people's concerns these days. She took a deep breath.

"Listen, I was tested years ago in school, and I haven't slept with anyone since then, like I told you, so you don't have to worry about catching anything from me."

The words seemed to add to the distance between them.

"I figured as much. You don't have anything to worry about in that respect either, from me, but still…"

Charlotte took a deep breath, and couldn't repress a smile, for some unknown reason. "I know. There are…other risks."

"You don't seem all that upset about it." EJ watched her smother the smile, and wondered at the curious response. Once Millie had forgotten her pill and had nearly had a heart attack when she remembered. It had taken EJ days to calm her down. But Charlotte didn't seem angry or panicked that he'd forgotten to protect her.

"Well, you know, I guess I'm not. Chances are nothing happened. I heard once that the chances of getting pregnant are really pretty slim, statistically speaking, you know, so many people try for months and years, so it's unlikely that one time will result in a pregnancy, though that does happen, of course…" She took a deep breath, trying to stem the nervous babble that just seemed to spout.

"I think I'm probably at that safe time of the month, though I can check for sure later. But even if something did happen, I guess I'm okay with it."

The fact surprised her as much as anyone, and she continued, talking to herself as much as to him.

"I never thought I'd want to have a baby by myself, in fact, I always wanted to make sure I never repeated my mother's mistakes. But I wouldn't do what she did. I wouldn't give up my baby. It would be mine, and we would be our own little family. I wouldn't be alone anymore, and neither would he or she. I'd make sure of it."

He saw something flicker deep in her eyes as she spoke the words and he leaned in, kissing her softly. It was the only thing he could think of to do, and there was only one thing he could say.

"You wouldn't be by yourself. I wouldn't leave you alone."

He meant it. He'd made a mistake, and he would take responsibility for it. But was there more than that going on here? He fell back to the pillows, processing what had happened, and how the hell he could have let it. He'd never slipped up like this once before—never—and he didn't know what to feel.

It had only been a day, and everything in his life had changed. He wasn't the kind of guy to abandon his responsibilities—but wasn't that exactly what he'd done with Millie and his family? What of the carefree lifestyle he enjoyed? Was he ready to give that up? Did he love Charlotte, or were they just dealing with the moment?

All questions he couldn't answer right now. He cast a glance at Charlotte. She seemed unperturbed. Cool as a cucumber.

"I guess we'll just have to wait and see, but I think we should still strive to be, uh, careful from now on. The situation isn't exactly uncomplicated at the moment."

She propped herself up on her elbow, staring down at him. "Okay." She leaned down, flicking her tongue over a flat brown nipple. "So there's going to be a 'from now on,' huh?"

He couldn't believe the effect she had on him, and his dick twitched in response to her caress.

"I think I'd like to see what could happen once we get out of all of this mess." It was a nice, noncommittal answer.

"Me, too." She yawned, curling into him, and wrapping herself around him in way that made him feel in a way he never really had before. Did he love her? Was that possible? He didn't know, but whatever they had, for now, it was enough.

EJ STEPPED FROM the shower, his body tensing in immediate alert. He heard noises in the kitchen, looked across the room and saw that Charlotte was still asleep. Someone was in the house.

As he reached for the gun he'd left on the table by the bed, Charlotte's eyes popped open and he quickly lifted a finger to his lips, signaling her to be quiet. There was another rattling sound from downstairs, and she slid to the side of the bed, grabbing a robe he'd put out for her and quickly donning it.

EJ whispered for her to stay put and he slid from the room, hugging the wall as he made his way down the hall that looked down over an enormous great room, with its two-story vaulted ceiling and floor-to-ceiling view of the Atlantic coastline. He heard another clash and figured whoever was down there didn't know the house was occupied or didn't care, because they weren't being particularly quiet. It sounded like they were looking for something.

Sidling down the steps, he slipped quietly to the corner of the room by the kitchen, and caught sight of Charlotte standing in the doorway of the main bedroom, watching him closely, his cell phone gripped tightly in her hand.

While he wished she would stay put, he appreciated having her at his back, if only to dial 911.

It was then that he heard the familiar spitting of *"SugarHoneyIcedTea!"* that followed a huge clash of pans, and he swung around the corner, letting the gun fall back to his side with a whoosh of relief as he met the beautiful jade glance of his little sister, Grace.

Grace was the only one he knew who spelled out "shit" as a harmless acronym when she wanted to curse. Like his mom, Grace was a southern lady, though recently she'd been proving herself as one hell of a businesswoman as well. He grinned at her, setting his gun safely on the granite counter and pulling her into a bear hug.

"EJ! You scared me half to death." She caught her breath, laughing as he squeezed her, pulling her up off her feet as he'd always done since he was able.

"Same back atcha, little sister. Didn't you see my car?"

"I did. But when I came in, I called your name, looked around and didn't see anyone, and figured you were out fishing or something."

He must have been in the shower or sleeping like the dead. Luckily he and Charlotte hadn't been up to anything more noisy.

Grace eyed the gun on the counter. "Is there a reason you were on high alert?" She studied him. "And while you're welcome anytime, I'm a little surprised to find you here."

EJ looked back over his shoulder, wondering where Charlotte was; it hit him that she might think he was still downstairs with a burglar. He walked to the doorway to signal to her that it was okay, but she wasn't there anymore. She'd gone back into the room, apparently.

He assumed she'd heard their conversation and knew everything was okay. Ironically, the one thing he didn't want right now was more cops showing up at the door. Not until he had Charlotte out of the line of fire for last night's shooting.

"Uh, Gracie, I'm not here alone."

His sister arched up one well-groomed eyebrow.

"Really? That's news." She looked discreetly over

his shoulder. "Who's the lucky girl who finally dragged you away from your computer?"

"She was a suspect." He held his hand up as the brow reached higher. "Was. I've been investigating her, but things got complicated, and then they got dangerous. I couldn't think of anywhere else safe to go last night."

"You know you're always welcome, EJ. You don't even have to ask." She looked toward the doorway again before meeting his serious look with her own. "But I take it this is some serious trouble?"

"Her home was broken into, her brother's missing, and an officer was shot last night. Then some guy tried to grab her but luckily I got there in time. I want to stay out of sight until I know what's going on."

Grace's hand flew to her lips, her eyes dark with concern.

"Shot by whom?"

"We have to find out."

"And they could still be after her? After you?"

"It's very possible. Probable." He met her eyes. "If I'd known you would be here, I wouldn't have come. You know I'd never put you—"

"Oh, EJ," she said, cutting him off. She knew what he was going to say. She always did. "I'm not worried about me. Someone shot at you?"

Her arms were back around him tightly, and he knew he'd scared her. He set her back, his hands on her shoulders, tipping his forehead next to hers.

"It's okay. I didn't even get a scratch."

"I hate this."

"It's part of the job."

"I know. I can still hate it. Sometimes I wish you were still running Beaumont, instead of me."

He didn't bother hiding his shock. "What do you mean? You're kicking ass down there. No one's going to argue your leadership."

She laughed lightly. "No one except Jordan."

EJ fought the urge to smile, knowing his kid sister would not appreciate it. Jordan Davis was her teenage love, and the man she almost married. But Jordan was a traditional kind of guy who didn't envision his wife getting an MBA—from a school up north, no less—or running one of the largest shipping companies in the U.S. Grace had done both. And she would do more, EJ knew.

Since Grace had taken over leadership of the company, and Jordan had bought a spot on the board, sparks had flown between them again, but EJ knew Grace could handle it. But just in case she couldn't, EJ would handle Jordan himself. He liked the guy— and he believed Jordan's feelings for Grace were genuine—but no one was going to crush his little sister's dreams or deny her talents, not even a man who claimed to love her.

"Well, he just has to get used to the idea, and he's only one vote."

"I worry he'll sway the board."

"Don't worry. Just do your job. It'll work out. I've been hearing rave reviews. You've been the shot in the arm that the old place needed."

"Really?"

Her worried brow cleared, and she smiled, her eyes on something—someone—past his shoulder. He turned to see Charlotte, still dressed in the robe and looking a little tired, but so beautiful that he forgot himself for a moment and stared. Grace cleared her throat, and EJ saw the patches of color stain Charlotte's cheeks, and shook himself out of it.

He crossed the kitchen, taking Charlotte's hand in his and bringing her in, keenly aware of his sister's sharp observation.

"I'm sorry, darlin'—this is Grace, my sister. We were just catching up." He looked at Grace. "This is Charlotte Gerard. A…friend."

Grace stepped forward, hand out, her smile genuine. EJ knew his sister was probably curious, and worried, but she'd never forget her manners.

"Morning, Charlotte. I hear you've had a tough couple days. Well, you two are welcome here as long as you need to be. I'm just here for the day. I figured I could work from here and get away from the office for a change." She looked at EJ. "How about some breakfast?"

"I'll cook."

"I was working on it."

"So I heard. But I'll do it. Let me just see what

you've got here." He looked through the paper grocery bag, pulling out Danish and eggs, sausage and fruit. Not bad, though Grace was not exactly known for her culinary skills. She'd probably burn the fruit.

"Um, EJ?" Charlotte broke into the easy back-and-forth between sister and brother, and he smiled, wanting her to feel comfortable.

"Yeah, darlin'?"

"I should get dressed, but all I had with me was the dress, and that's ruined. And I need to make some phone calls—people are expecting me this morning. I'm already late for several appointments. And Phoebe. I don't know how I am going to explain the dress, but I have to do something."

He read the slight embarrassment in her features, and anxiety about missing her obligations. He wanted to just cross the room and hold her, kiss her and let her know she could relax.

"It's probably better if you stay out of contact for the moment, Charlotte. You can square things when you get back." He looked at Grace, stemming any objections from Charlotte. "We had to leave in a hurry—do you have anything here Charlotte could borrow?"

Grace nodded and took Charlotte by the arm, leading her from the kitchen. "I'm very sure I do. Let's go look and leave EJ in the kitchen to work his magic."

EJ smiled, watching Charlotte's hips hugged by the fabric of the robe as she walked from the room and he wished he could be working his magic in the bedroom instead, but he was better off making break-fast for the moment. Easier said than done. His mind returned to the passionate encounter they'd shared just hours ago, how she'd tempted him, and how he lost control, coming so hard that he'd seen stars for a few seconds.

And maybe forging a connection with this woman that was going to last much longer than he'd ever intended.

Arranging items on the counter, he tested the thought again that he and Charlotte could have con-ceived a child, and found it only left him with a warm sense of…something. He liked the feeling. He liked Charlotte—more than liked—and he liked the connection they had. He frowned then, cracking eggs into a bowl.

But what if she had more doubts in the clear light of day? What if her easygoing attitude changed once everything was said and done?

Well, they'd talk. For now, it was best to let sleeping dogs lie. But when he went out, buying condoms was one of the things on his must-do list. While there were more important things to think about than sex at the moment, obviously, he couldn't believe they'd resist each other for long. Especially if the stirrings he felt down yonder while watching her exit the room were any indication.

9

CHARLOTTE WASN'T SURE HOW to deal with the sudden appearance of EJ's sister. She was tired, a little sore and sticky from making love with EJ, and unsure what Grace really thought of finding her brother in the house with a strange woman.

But Grace Beaumont was the epitome of friendliness and polite to a fault, searching through the dressers and closets until she pulled out several selections from which Charlotte hoped something would fit. It wasn't hard to see that Grace was several willowy sizes smaller than she was.

"Hopefully you'll find something there that you like. It's mostly summer clothes and dresses. The espadrilles are well-worn, and hopefully will be comfortable until you can get your own clothes."

"I appreciate it." She looked down at the robe, then back up at Grace. "Everything has been such a blur."

Grace's expression was sympathetic. "It sounds like you've been through the ringer, you poor thing. Last night must have been very frightening for you."

Charlotte's head snapped up. "You know?"

Grace nodded. "EJ told me, not much detail, but enough to know you are both involved in something pretty awful, and…"

Grace smoothed the bed covers, busying her hands while letting her thoughts drift off.

"And?" Charlotte prompted.

"Well, I hate to pry, but it's obvious only one bed-room was used last night."

Charlotte felt the blush travel from the roots of her hair to the bottoms of her feet, and wasn't exactly sure what to say.

"I'm sorry, Charlotte—this is none of my busi-ness. I just worry about him, and he, well…you must be very special."

"Why do you say that?"

"EJ wouldn't just bring anyone here, to a family place, even if he was in danger. And besides—" Grace smiled faintly as she looked Charlotte in the eye "—I could see something in the way he looks at you. When did you two meet?"

"Just a few days ago."

"Oh."

"But we talked online quite a bit before that."

"On the computer?" The hint of disbelief in Grace's voice snuck through even though Charlotte bet she was doing her best to be nonjudgmental. She was just worried about her brother, and that was one thing Charlotte could very well relate to.

"Yes, I run an online…business." She didn't know

how Grace would react to knowing she read tarot cards regarding people's love lives, so decided to generalize. "EJ came to the site pretending to be a client, though he really was just investigating me...." She shrugged helplessly. "But I'm not guilty of anything. It's complicated."

"Do you...love him?"

"It's a little soon for that, I think."

Charlotte looked away as she saw Grace's features lighten. But Charlotte knew that if she were honest, her heart had already traveled a long way toward loving EJ. Time didn't make a difference to her when it came to those kinds of things—she'd loved Ronny before she'd even met him. But she also realized that most people thought love was dependent on a clock or a calendar, and she didn't want to make Grace feel uncomfortable. She was being so nice, considering she'd just come here for a quiet respite from work only to discover her brother hiding out with a strange woman in her home.

Still, even if Charlotte did love EJ, she wasn't about to share it with anyone else when she hadn't even told EJ. Especially his sister who, while obviously being a very nice person, seemed relieved that things were not serious between them. Though she was sure Grace was too polite to say so, Charlotte could feel the awkward tension between them across the room. They were just very different people shoved together in a strange situation.

"Thanks for being so nice, and sharing your clothes. I don't want to seem ungrateful, but I really need to get in the shower." Charlotte smiled in what she hoped was a friendly, casual way.

"Yes, of course. I'm sorry. I guess I'll see you down at breakfast?"

"I'll be down shortly, but don't wait for me if you're hungry."

Charlotte walked to the shower, relieved to have the interaction with EJ's sister over with for the moment. As she stepped into the beautifully tiled shower, the hot water sprayed down on her as she realized with a deep sense of resignation that it might be the least of the troubles facing her in the days ahead.

"WHAT DID YOU FIND?"

Ian crossed the lab, pulling a chair up next to Sarah, hoping whatever she'd found was good news. He didn't know where EJ was—no one knew.

EJ had called once to check on Nate Donovan and update Ian. Though the man who'd grabbed Charlotte was long gone by the time they'd arrived, EJ was able to give them a name to track down. Ian had put that in Sarah's capable hands while he'd gone home to check on Sage, who was teetering on the edge of childbirth and sanity. Ian felt pulled in so many directions that he could barely keep up.

So at this point, though they could find EJ if they tried hard enough, he was more inclined to trust his friend's instincts and help where he could. They'd been friends and colleagues too long for Ian to cast doubt now. But it was clear from the expression on Sarah's face that she didn't have good news.

"EJ may be in much deeper trouble than he suspected."

She turned the screen toward him, lowering her voice—a sure signal that whatever she'd found, she'd skipped over a few federal computer privacy laws to do it.

"Tell me."

"Okay. Well, I tracked down the numbers we found on the documents they took out of Ronny Fulsom's place, and they led to offshore accounts in the Caymans—big money that's been accumulated bits at a time. The accounts were listed in the brother's name with Charlotte listed second on the account."

"Of which she has no idea, as EJ would have it," Ian said.

"EJ might be wrong."

"Not likely."

"There's always a first time," Sarah said sharply.

Ian studied Sarah, who was being more pit-bull-ish than usual.

"Why are you so down on this woman? So quick to believe she's guilty, when it's obvious EJ doesn't think so?" he asked.

Sarah didn't meet Ian's eyes, and continued tapping keys and studying the screen as she spoke, shrugging. "I don't know if she's guilty or not, but I know how men get around a woman they're attracted to. Common sense can go out the window."

Ian grinned. "And women don't suffer that affliction?"

"Not me."

Ian coughed to cover his laugh, deciding not to mention how mooney-eyed his tough-girl colleague got when her husband-to-be walked into the room. He turned his attention back to the discussion at hand.

"I'm surprised you could get that kind of information from the banks—private accounts are usually kept that way, even from the law unless there's a lot of pressure from the government."

Sarah arched an eyebrow, and looked only at the screen. "I went through channels. You're right, they didn't cooperate."

"So then you went around the channels, I take it?"

She nodded, her mouth quirking at the corner. Ian shouldn't encourage her, but he knew she'd find something. If something was on a network somewhere and Sarah couldn't find it, then it couldn't be found. The things she could do while sitting at a computer always astounded him, and he was frequently thankful he'd gone with his gut and hired her—an inexperienced, untrained hacker who'd simply been one of his informants—to join their team.

Sarah had become one of the best cops he'd ever

known. She was deeply committed to the work and to the people with whom she worked, which was probably why she was so prickly about EJ's interest in Charlotte Gerard. She was feeling protective. So was he. But he also trusted EJ to do the right thing.

"I was also able to hack into some of the transfers using previous theft victims' information, and they match up."

"So we have hard evidence that the money stolen from SexyTarot.com clients was deposited in these accounts?"

"After some rather lame attempts at laundering, yeah. If it was her brother, he passed it through a few points before it was deposited, but that was easy to trace. He's obviously not a pro. But we still don't know if it's just him. Her name is here, too."

"Covering his own ass?"

"Could be. Or could be she's pulling one over on EJ."

"I find that hard to believe. He's hardly that easy to pull one over on."

Sarah shrugged. "Men in lust will do strange things."

Ian had to agree, remembering his own experiences crossing the line with Sage. To say their beginning was rocky was an understatement—as a convicted felon, Sage had definitely been off limits to him, a federal investigator in charge of her parole at the time. But the attraction they'd had was stronger than the rules that would keep him from her, and a dangerous threat to her from a former lover, a mastermind of a hacker, had deepened their attraction.

There was no reason to think EJ wasn't in the same boat. Suddenly, Ian was kicking himself—hard—for letting his best friend walk away the night before. And he had no idea where he was now.

"So, any ideas who was coming out shooting last night and who that gun belonged to?" Ian asked.

"Well, I'd say it looks like Ronny and his sister—if she's involved—managed to rip off the wrong person this time. There was one large score, the last entry on the account. The name I was able to trace the license to was an alias, so I'm running it through the federal databases to see if we get a match. My guess is, from the hit on the house and what EJ reported last night, that whoever it is has a lot of resources. Not people you want to rip off."

"You think it's someone in organized crime?"

"Just a guess, but the ballistics from the shooting last night would seem to back it up. High-end weaponry, not stuff your average teenagers use for random drive-bys. And untraceable," she added.

Ian peered through the glass, watching the morning buzz as the offices swung into high gear. "Then EJ could be right about an inside leak."

No cop liked to admit it, but organized crime's tentacles reached far and wide, and sometimes found their way a little too easily into law enforcement agencies. A dirty cop could make a lot of money and send his kids to college a lot easier just by making a few phone calls here and there, or by overlooking things from time to time.

"Could be. Or they just could have had eyes in the neighborhood. Safest place for EJ and his new girl-friend could be right here, but it's hard to say."

Ian looked at Sarah speculatively. "You're worried about him."

She bit her lip, her expression not changing much as she studied the screen. Sarah was such a tough cookie, but Ian knew she was close to EJ. He'd actually been surprised when they'd ended up only as friends.

"Aren't you?" she countered.

"Yeah."

She spat out a curse, a mild one, her eyes on the screen. "We've got a name match on the guy from the bar, now we can really do some digging."

It didn't take long. Ian didn't recognize the name that Sarah scratched on a piece of paper, and he paced, walking back to the other side of the lab, strategizing as Sarah's hands flew over the keyboard.

"Man, oh, man."

Her whisper pulled him back to her side, and Ian looked at the screen, his stomach dropping out a little.

The guy with the gun was linked with Lou Maloso.

Sarah sat back blowing out a breath. "This is just

un-friggin-believable. The putz stole from one of the biggest crime bosses on the eastern seaboard. He swiped twenty grand right off of his credit card. Holy mama."

Sarah talked aloud to herself while she worked, a habit she'd never quite been able to break, but she was echoing Ian's thoughts. He watched her as she leaned in, her fingers running furiously over the keyboard, muttering to herself while she honed in.

"And there's the final piece—it all fits."

"Show me," Ian said.

Sarah had hacked into SexyTarot.com, and looked at a customer file. All the people who had signed on for readings were listed, with their credit card information under the registration page. It was basically secure, unless you could hack your way in, as Sarah had done, but that would leave evidence behind. But if someone had Charlotte's laptop with her user name and password checked off to be saved, as many people did, for quick access, then anyone, including her brother, could have gotten that account information.

Ian scanned the list, wondering what it was Sarah was looking for. EJB showed up several times, but then he turned his gaze to where Sarah's finger was pointing to on the screen—the user name: LOU52.

So it looked like one of the major mafioso on the east coast had signed up for tarot readings about his love life. Ian shook his head; it would almost be laughable if it weren't EJ's neck on the chopping block right now. Maloso might not be after EJ, but he was after Charlotte and her brother, and EJ was in the way.

"I'm calling EJ now." Ian ran a hand over his face. Wherever his best friend was, Ian hoped they were well out of sight.

CHARLOTTE FELT AS IF she were in a movie, or some other place that wasn't quite real as she and EJ walked along a beach that seemed to stretch out forever.

She'd never seen any of the National Seashore before, even though another section of it in Cape Cod had only been hours away from her when she lived in New Hampshire. It was wild and sprawling, and she laughed as the water chased her bare feet. The tide was coming in, and she stopped, frozen in awe as she saw horses calmly chewing on greens just a few yards ahead of them.

"I'd heard about this, but I can't believe I'm seeing it."

"Yeah. They're amazing, aren't they? Once used by settlers here, but left on their own they've reverted to their wild state."

"They're small, like ponies."

"The diet they get here isn't great, so their size is smaller to adapt. Marsh grasses and such. The caretakers keep the herd small, too, to help avoid them destroying the area, trampling and eating everything."

Charlotte frowned. "They kill them?"

"No, in Virginia, in Chincoteague, it's a yearly event to go to the pony penning—haven't you heard of it? It's usually in the news even in Norfolk."

"I may have, but I don't recall."

"It's quite the event. They have 'saltwater cowboys' who corral the herd when they swim across a channel at slack tide, with everyone watching, and they take the foals and auction them off to new owners. The proceeds go to various groups, and the new owners are held to strict standards for humane ownership of their horses."

"They don't do that here in Maryland?"

"No, the herd had grown here, and they are using some dart-injected contraceptives to prevent more reproduction."

"Oh. That's good."

They were suddenly quiet, the talk of contraception reminding them of last night.

"I'm sorry Charlotte. You have so much on your mind as it is. I hate adding to it."

"I'm not worried, EJ. Except about you."

He moved in front of her. "I told you, you don't have to worry about me. I wouldn't leave you high and dry, or any child I may have fathered, either."

"I'm not your responsibility, EJ, nor your obligation. I don't want your money, I want—" Irritated with herself and almost saying much more than she wanted to reveal just yet, she yanked her hand from his and walked away. He was by her side again in a second, grabbing her hand back and swinging her around to face him.

"Dammit, I didn't mean to make it sound like that. I care about you, Charlotte, and I just want you to know—*dammit!*"

The cell phone in his pocket rang, interrupting his point. He snapped it open with a force that had her raising her eyebrows as he turned and took the call in hushed tones.

He cared for her. About her. What did that mean, exactly? She wished she knew what he'd been about to say. She saw his shoulders raise—whatever he was hearing on the phone it wasn't good news.

He clicked the phone shut, looking around them, and slipped his arm around her, pulling her close as if to cuddle her—or hide her against him—as they headed back toward the house at a pace that was much faster than the leisurely one they'd enjoyed before.

"EJ? What is it?"

He didn't answer her question, but hurried her back to the house, closing the sliding glass doors behind them and scanning the beach and the horizon before yanking the curtain over. He noticed Grace's car was gone; she must have left while they were out on their walk, discretion being a major value in Grace's world. EJ was glad she'd gone back to the city, now that he had a better idea what they were dealing with. He didn't want his sister anywhere near the danger he was in right now, and he was regretting he'd come to her home in the first place.

"EJ, you're freaking me out—what's going on?"

"Do you have a client named Lou Maloso?"

She thought for a moment—LOU52—and she did see his full name on her registration list.

"Yes, actually, how did—"

"Oh, Jesus, Charlotte. He's a mobster."

A what? She didn't utter the words, but the question must have shown in the expression on her face. EJ planted his hands on his hips, nodding.

"Gangster, mafia, wiseguy, organized crime—whatever they're calling it these days. He's one of the main men on the east coast."

She blinked, unable to really believe what she was hearing.

"He didn't come across like a criminal. He was just a nice man who'd lost his girlfriend, and he wondered if he would find anyone again anytime soon. He…gave me a generous tip."

He regarded her with open incredulity, and she sank into the nearest chair, trying to match up the pleasant and innocent conversations she'd had with Lou—who'd always been a complete gentleman—with what EJ was telling her.

"There has to be some mistake."

"Ian and Sarah have uncovered the trail—the cops found documents with what ended up being bank account numbers in Ronny's apartment. With your name on the accounts as well, by the way—illegal, offshore accounts. The man who tried to grab you last night? He's a known associate of Lou Maloso. Worse, the same money trail shows that whoever's been ripping off the customers that come to the Sexy-Tarot Web site—probably Ronny—ripped off Maloso, too. Not a good scene. These are not people to mess with."

"But why would they be trying to get me instead of Ronny then?"

EJ sat next to Charlotte, pulling her forward, his hand curled around the back of her neck as he nestled her face in his shoulder, and rubbed the soft skin at her nape.

"Well, there are a couple possibilities. One, they need you to find Ronny, who is probably in hiding—so you are bait. They probably also think you may have been in on it, or know where he is, or why the money was stolen. Then, it could be that Ronny set you up to take the fall, and he ran off with the money."

He felt her tense against him, heard her soft gasp when he spoke the second option, but he held her in place.

"I'm sorry, darlin', but either way, there's a heap of trouble going on here, and I'm not letting you out of my sight until it's settled."

"But what are we going to do?"

She pulled back, looking at him with desperate

eyes, and all he wanted to do was wipe the hurt from her expression, to ease the pain of her brother's betrayal and make her feel safe. She shook her head, her voice just a whisper, "We have to help him, EJ. They'll kill him if they find him, won't they?"

"It's a likely possibility. And it's also likely, depending on what the whole story is, that they'll keep coming after you, too. These people don't take things like this sitting down."

"How much…how much was stolen?"

"Twenty thousand from the credit card that Maloso used for the site, and then the money was converted to cash and laundered out of the country. It's not a lot of money, relatively speaking, considering the millions of dollars that organized crime is involved with every day, but it's a personal insult. Maloso may feel that you made a fool of him—he came to you on a very personal level and was betrayed. He's not going to let it go."

"Lou should know that I wouldn't do anything like that."

"Charlotte, these are not a trusting bunch of people. They live in a world where your best friend or even a family member can be your worst enemy."

She made a face. "I know—I'm not completely out of it, I have watched *The Sopranos*." She huffed a breath. "So what do we do? What's next?"

"We stay out of sight."

"But Ronny—"

"Ronny is on his own."

Tears stung her eyes and her chin firmed in resistance to them and him. "I'm not accepting that."

"You don't have a choice."

"There's always a choice. I'm not going to sit here while my brother is out there somewhere in danger, and I could be helping."

"How are you going to help, Charlotte? Exactly what can you do, except maybe get yourself killed?"

She pondered the idea, wondering herself, until the obvious answer emerged.

"I can talk to Lou."

"Pardon me?"

"I can talk to him through the Web site—explain, let him know what happened, even return the money." She sat up straight, her mind racing, convinced she'd discovered a way out. "I know what you're saying about him, but really, EJ, he's a very nice man, at least with me. He'll listen."

EJ just stared, first in disbelief and then his own mind started working over the situation. Doing something was better than just sitting here doing nothing, waiting for the next shoe to drop. Could this work?

Stranger things were possible, and talking to the crime boss over the Internet wouldn't pose any threat—as long as they did it from a safe location. No doubt Maloso had resources that could track them in seconds, especially if he had mules on the inside, and so EJ would have to make sure they were somewhere untrackable. And he thought he might know exactly the place.

While he processed the idea, he took in Charlotte's brightened eyes, the flush in her cheeks, the red bloom of her mouth. His chest tightened with desire, which stunned him—this was hardly the time for sex, but as her hand settled on his thigh, squeezing lightly, he hardened immediately and couldn't take his eyes off of her lips. She shifted closer—was she actually thinking about using wiles on him, seducing him to convince him of her plan?

It was working, even though he'd already considered actually going along with her zany idea.

Charlotte leaned in, her breath sweet on his skin and he closed his eyes, trying to focus on anything but the effect she was having.

"It could work, EJ. Please let me try."

Dammit, her mouth dragged down the line of his neck, and he swallowed, trying to keep his wits about him, but images of their coupling the night before assaulted him as her hand moved higher on his thigh, and he groaned, turning his head to capture her mouth in a hot kiss, aborting all conversation for the moment as he pushed her back on the sofa, sliding his hand under the soft material of the sweater she'd borrowed from Grace and closing over the hot, satiny skin of her breast.

He nudged a knee between hers, endlessly grateful she was wearing a skirt, and pushed his thigh up tight between her legs, murmuring approval as she locked her legs around him, moaning in pleasure and offering her mouth to his for another kiss.

Before things went where they were inevitably heading, he reached into his jacket pocket, pulling out the small box of condoms he'd picked up at the gas station earlier—there were only three, which seemed paltry considering how he felt like he needed to get in between Charlotte's legs at every opportunity.

His breath was short as she wound herself around him, and her hands loosened his belt, sliding his zipper down and freeing him. If she wanted to seduce him, he was more than willing. He was a goner, maybe in more ways that he ever expected. Covering himself quickly, he reached down, pulling the material of her panties roughly aside, and entered her in one hard thrust, giving in to the basic instincts she'd stoked to life and losing his breath at how her body hugged his, how right it all felt.

"God, Charlotte, what you do to me…"

He started to move, catching every sigh, every kiss that she offered him, knowing he would do whatever it took in the world to protect her, to make her happy.

He didn't know what that all meant, or maybe he just wasn't ready to deal with it yet. Either way, he knew he would support her in contacting Lou and

trying to help her brother, a plan forming in the back
of his mind, even as he lost himself in the heaven of
her embrace.

10

"So who exactly is Jennie Snow?"

Charlotte looked out the window, but she wasn't an idiot—she had seen the slight flicker, EJ's veiled gaze when he said they were going to meet this Jennie person. She tried breathing deeply to loosen the knot of unfamiliar emotion that settled in her chest when EJ had mentioned Jennie Snow. Charlotte had known almost immediately that he knew this woman more than professionally.

"I told you—she works for the National Institute of Justice's Mapping and Analysis for Public Safety. She used to be part of the Department of Justice, where I worked years ago."

"And she makes maps of crimes?"

Charlotte was stymied at how any of this would be helpful to them; unless EJ was just looking for an excuse to see Jennie Snow. The odd thought pinched her, and she swatted it away. EJ was not that kind of man; but there was more to his relationship with her than he was letting on.

"Well, it's more interactive than that. They do

map crime occurrences, but they also use GIS and GPS—computer mapping technology—to locate trends, for instance, tracking gang growth and activity, or finding connections between types of crimes. They might study areas that are particularly prone to crime—they research just about everything now. Anything can be put on a map, tracked by satellites, et cetera. They keep track of major criminal figures and their actions, and try to predict future trends. It's really very cool."

"So how does this help us?"

"Well, Jennie's particular area is mapping organized crime activity on the east coast. She'll have the most up-to-date information on where Maloso is, what his people have been up to, and we'll also be able to use untraceable computers to contact him."

"But if he finds out we're contacting him through the government, he won't talk to me. Can't we just go to an Internet café or something? Use a friend's computer?"

EJ shook his head resolutely as he descended down the northern end of the Chesapeake Bay Bridge, the section at the top of the bay that sent him in the direction of Annapolis, Baltimore and D.C.

"If Maloso gets chilled, then that's fine. We'll have more information on him than we had before, and there's no way we're going to make any attempt to contact him where his people can get you out in the open."

Charlotte didn't say a word, but suddenly her plan didn't seem to be going quite the way she'd imagined. She'd been thrilled and surprised when EJ had said she had a good idea, but now she wasn't so sure.

"What if he just gets more angry? Won't this confirm his sense that I've betrayed him? If he thinks I'm working with the cops?"

EJ shrugged. "That's a chance we have to take—it won't put us in any worse of a position than we're in now."

Charlotte bit her lip, trying to restrain her angry response, but not quite succeeding.

"And what about Ronny, EJ? He doesn't have government protection. Lou can get him—maybe already has him."

She received no response for a moment, and when she did, it wasn't the one she expected.

"Charlotte, aren't you angry with your brother at all? He used you, could have ended up sending you to prison or getting you killed, and at the very least has disrupted your life and the business you were trying to build. Doesn't that bother you at all? What he's done?"

Charlotte shook her head.

"I don't know. I can't seem to be really angry with him, I'm so worried. He's had a hard time of it. He needs me, my support. He wouldn't have hurt me on purpose—he just doesn't…think sometimes."

EJ's voice was gentle, and she felt his hand on her

thigh, squeezing softly in a nonsexual way that made her vision blur again. It would have been easier if he just kept picking on Ronny.

"I know it's hard to accept, but you've only known him for a short while, right? A few years? And in that time, is this the first time he's caused you pain or inconvenience?"

Charlotte straightened her back. "He's been thoughtless from time to time, but it's because he was never taught otherwise. The couple who adopted him kicked him out and never cared about him. And he always apologizes when he steps over the line, and he is very good to me in general."

"Have you ever felt unsafe around him?"

She shook her head resolutely. "No, never."

"His friends?"

She remembered how she'd asked Ronny not to bring some of his friends to her apartment; they'd looked at her like fresh meat, and she had always been nervous when they hung around, and worried they might have come back when her brother wasn't there.

"Sometimes. But he can't be held responsible for how his friends are."

"Sure he can. He's a grown man, Charlotte, not a child, and a man has to be held responsible for his actions, and for the people he chooses to hang around with."

EJ was quiet for a moment, as if he were thinking how to say whatever came next, and she just waited.

"I know you love him, and I know he's your only family, but you have to accept that he's not a child. He knows what he's doing, and this time he didn't do a thoughtless thing—he did a very dangerous thing that took a whole lot of thought and planning. And he put you in danger's way without so much as a second glance."

Charlotte railed against the words, her voice raising in her brother's defense.

"I refuse to believe that. There has to be more to it, something we don't know."

"Maybe. But we have enough evidence to arrest him, and if we find him, which I hope we do, before Maloso's goons find him, then I'm going to have to take him in. You understand that, right?"

She said nothing.

"It's up to the courts, but he could be looking at a hefty sentence."

She felt her chest clench. If Ronny went to jail, she'd be alone in the world again. But she couldn't expect EJ to feel about her brother like she did. She looked around desperately, trying to stem the overwhelming wash of emotion that threatened to break free, fixed her gaze on the spots from dried rain on the window and began counting under her breath.

"What are you doing?"

"What?"

"You're mumbling numbers."

"I, uh…I was counting."

"Counting what?"

She shrugged, not wanting to get into it. "Stuff."

"You've done that before. Why?"

"It's just something I do."

"To get a sense of control back?"

She was surprised at his insight; most people just thought her habit was weird, or if they were kind, quirky.

"I guess."

"I used to have a friend who did something similar. Every time we were on stakeouts he would do fractions out loud. He said it helped him pass the time, but I think it was also a response to stress."

Charlotte wasn't sure what to say, so she said nothing.

"Did I make you feel so stressed, Charlotte, that you had to start counting? If so, I'm sorry. But I need to be honest with you, so you know what's coming."

"I understand that. It breaks my heart, but I know you have a job to do."

"It's more than that, Charlotte. Don't you see?" He stopped at the red light—they'd hit some lunch hour traffic behind construction, and would probably be stuck for a few minutes. Dropping his hands from the wheel, he reached over, turning her face to his, looking at her intently.

"I'm not trying to hurt you, I just want you to see that none of this is your fault, honey. No matter how much you believe you could have seen what was coming, and even if you could, Ronny made his own choices. He's in control of his own destiny, not you."

She hadn't really thought of that before, though it seemed so simple. How could she be so arrogant as to think she was in control of someone else's life? Their choices? Her mind reeled with the new realization, but part of her resisted. She still felt it had to be more complicated than that. Didn't family help out each other, try to share the load? Wasn't it too easy to just back away, saying she had no responsibility? But before she could say so, EJ continued, his voice tight with barely disguised anger toward her brother.

"He's the luckiest guy in the world finding out he had a sister like you, and then he uses you like this?" EJ blew out a breath. "You met my sister, Grace?"

She nodded. It's not likely she could have forgotten over less than twelve hours.

"She can drive me crazy, but I would throw myself in front of a truck before I'd hurt her like your brother has hurt you. And while I understand that you find it hard to be angry with him, that's okay because I can assure you I am angry enough for both of us."

Charlotte was stunned, seeing the conviction of his words in his beautiful green eyes. Only moments before she'd been feeling hollow and abandoned, but now she realized what EJ was saying. He cared. He was standing up for her. He wasn't just angry at her brother like a cop after a criminal, but because Ronny had hurt her.

It was a stunning realization that no one—ever— had fought for her before. She'd always been the one to do the fighting, the one who protected. And now here was EJ, so angry with Ronny because he'd hurt her...the idea filled her with happiness, and confusion. She didn't want him angry at her brother, and yet she was warmed by having someone stand up for her so adamantly.

"You have a right to be angry, Charlotte. In fact, you should be angry. Maybe Ronny needs to feel that from you to get the point. When people hurt us, even people we love, we have the right to let them know it. I know you're afraid of losing him, but maybe if you can find a way to have a healthier relationship, one where he's not always hurting you and you're not always making excuses for him, well, who knows? Prison isn't the end of the world."

Feeling as if she'd been released from the spell of her misery, Charlotte was grateful to EJ for so many things she couldn't even name. Hope laced her tone as she thought forward, leaving her black thoughts behind.

"You really think so?"

"I do."

EJ returned his attention to the wheel as traffic moved forward again, and they sat in silence for a little while longer.

"I wish I could take you to this little place in Annapolis—maybe after this mess is over with. They have the best crabcakes in the world, though I guess I'm being a traitor to my home state by saying so."

"One thing I've noticed since I've lived here is you folks do take your crab seriously."

EJ grinned, glad to move on from the more serious tenor of the discussion they'd been having.

She saw the sign for the exit that would take them to D.C. and settled back.

"I wish I'd remembered to bring my cards with me. I was so panicked that night, when everything happened, I didn't even realize I wouldn't be returning to my home."

"Do you think they might give you some insight into what's happening?"

She shrugged, feeling defensive even though there was nothing judgmental in his tone.

"I don't know—maybe—or they might just help me deal with it all."

"I have to admit, it was pretty interesting how you do that. You came up with a lot of really neat stuff when we were talking online—maybe some of it was closer to the mark than I was comfortable with."

Unsure if he was pandering, though he sounded perfectly sincere, she slanted a look in his direction.

"Yeah? Like what?"

"Like how you could be so detailed about what

turns me on, not just taking shots in the dark, but linking it to my personality. When you haven't met someone, that's a pretty interesting insight to have. Or how you advised me to be careful about playing things too fast and loose—that I might come up against something unexpected, something that would change my life, and that I should be careful."

Charlotte wasn't sure if she'd imagined the husky note of suggestion in his voice. She tried to play it casual.

"Well, I guess I did hit that nail on the head, considering everything you've been through the last few days."

"I don't think it's this situation that was unexpected, though I agree, it's been a surprising turn of events."

He paused, and she waited for him to continue, unable to take her eyes from his profile. He pulled smoothly into a parking spot, not looking at her, even as he killed the ignition. When he did meet her gaze, the undisguised emotion she saw there stole her breath, but not so much as the words that passed his lips,

"What is most unexpected, and what has probably changed my life, is how I am starting to feel about you."

EJ STEPPED INTO the group of offices where Jennie Snow had her little space within the massive complex and was relieved to have moved on from the car conversation. He might have revealed more than he wanted to, unsure of what his feelings actually were, but aware that Charlotte was beginning to mean something more than the other women he'd spent time with in the past few years.

Women like Jennie. He'd felt a little awkward calling her on business, when he'd spent the weekend in her bed less than a month ago.

She was a great woman, and he'd enjoyed being with her, but they usually just got together when he had reason to be in D.C., and neither of them expected anything else. Though he wasn't in the habit of having two women he'd been to bed with in the same room, there really wasn't much of an option. The best bet, he thought as he approached her corner by the window, was to keep everything on business.

That was going to be a little difficult, he realized, when he saw Jennie turn the corner and upon seeing him, light up and come at him with a big smile and arms extended. Jennie—whose original last name was not really Snow—was as Italian as the day is long, and it was just in her nature to be physically affectionate.

It was also in her nature to have a nasty temper, though thankfully he'd only witnessed that secondhand. His experiences with Jennie's passionate nature had always been much more friendly. But that was in the past, and he disengaged himself gently, stepping back and drawing Charlotte forward to stand next to him.

"Jennie, this is Charlotte Gerard, the woman I was telling you about on the phone."

He noted a stiffening of Charlotte's posture upon the introduction, and felt a little irritated. What did she expect? That he introduce her as his current lover? Jennie's outgoing nature extended to Charlotte as well, and she greeted her with just as much warmth, if not the hugs.

"Charlotte! What a gorgeous name. So romantic."

Jennie cast a knowing and somewhat teasing look in EJ's direction, and then hooked her arm through Charlotte's, walking toward her desk.

"So I hear you are having some trouble with Lou Maloso?" She shook her head. "Bad news, that one."

"So I gather." Charlotte finally spoke, and EJ realized he'd been holding his breath.

Jennie sat in her chair, and swept her hand toward two cheap vinyl chairs near her desk. "Please, sit. Tell me what I can do to help."

"Well, as I told you on the phone, we have good reason to believe Lou's men are after Charlotte. They may have her brother, and they could be trying to get Charlotte as more leverage against him, or they don't have the brother, and they figure Charlotte can tell them what they need to know."

"And that would be?"

"My brother, Ronny, stole from them. He probably had no idea who they were, and I'm sure he wouldn't have done it if he'd known—" EJ caught her eye, and she stopped, her shoulders slumping slightly. He put a hand on her shoulder to let her know he understood; old habits died hard.

"Anyway, I think I can talk to Lou and see if I can reason with him."

Jennie's velvet-black eyebrows shot up in surprise, then lowered in suspicion. "You know Lou Maloso? Personally?"

Charlotte nodded. EJ interjected, saving her the trouble of explaining.

"Charlotte reads tarot cards for an online service—insights and predictions about people's love lives and relationships." He smiled down at Charlotte. "She's amazing at it. Lou was one of her clients. She had no idea who he was—everything is by pseudonym, and he used an alias to pay."

Jennie shook her head, her well-manicured hand falling to the desk in a gesture of astonishment. Then she grinned, her dark, dark brown eyes lighting up.

"Lou Maloso going for tarot readings, eh? *Culo!* His mama is probably rolling in her grave, though the people from the old country have their own share of beliefs in spells and curses, and I guess some of it has carried forward."

"Some of the tarot's history originates in Italy, so maybe it's not so curious," Charlotte offered.

EJ interrupted, getting them back on track. "Can you share any of your current information on where Maloso might be?"

"I can see what I have. Not much recently, I don't think. He's been status quo for months, nothing much new going on, though someone did trace some movement to Virginia the other day—I guess that must have been connected to you somehow."

"We also need a secure connection where Charlotte can e-mail him and try to get him to meet her online."

"No problem. You can use my machine right here—I know it's safe."

"That would be great, Jennie. Thanks so much. But I don't want you crossing any lines for us. We don't want to put you in any danger."

EJ knew that this was all risky business for Jennie, though he couldn't share that with Charlotte. Very few people knew who Jennie really was, and it had to stay that way.

Jennie's real name had been Maria Castone, and she was the daughter of a major mafioso. Five years before, when her father and brother had been killed on orders from her uncle, she came to the government and offered testimony in exchange for protection and a job. They'd made a deal, and she'd been Jennie Snow ever since.

But instead of moving to some small town in Nebraska, Jennie had pushed for a "hide in plain sight" strategy, living in D.C. and using her skills to help take down the crime families she'd grown up with. Her life was always at risk, and always would be. EJ couldn't help but admire the work she did, and her willingness to help. He also knew she lived a life steeped in caution, and void of any close connections. She kept everyone at a distance, since getting close could cost her her life—or theirs.

"I'm fine, EJ. No worries. I'm happy to help. Work here has gotten so boring lately, I am glad to cross a line or two. Most of the funds and the attention go to the terrorism units now."

"Looking for new work?"

Jennie picked up a well-chewed pencil and bit into it, assessing EJ with a shrewd glance. "You offering?"

"I know someone who's looking. My unit is expanding—they're looking for some good people. Experienced people. I could put in a word for you—I think Ian would be very interested in someone with your skills and specialization."

Jennie smiled brightly. "We'll talk about that later, but maybe, yes, pass my name along. I'd appreciate that. It might be a good time for me to move. You know, career-wise."

Jennie's glance was a little too warm, and he broke the gaze, too aware of Charlotte's keen attention on their exchange.

"May we send that message now? Then I need to contact Ian, so I can let him know what's up."

Jennie stood, looking at her watch. "I have a meeting. Feel free to use this machine as long as you like, and just close down when you're done."

"Thanks. We'll need to check for responses, and then come back to do the session, if he agrees," EJ said.

"Just let me know what you need."

The words hung a little uncomfortably between them all, and then Jennie left, and Charlotte spoke directly.

"So how long were you two an item?"

EJ gestured for Charlotte to sit so that she could log into her e-mail.

"We were never an item. We just had a few dates. Nothing serious or steady," he said.

"Oh. You seem very close," Charlotte said softly.

Taking a deep breath, EJ decided to tend to the task at hand, and leave the conversation about Jennie behind. There really wasn't much more to say about his relationship with her to Charlotte, and he didn't really want to. Even if Jennie wasn't his lover anymore, and even if she wouldn't be in the future, she was still a friend.

"Can you log into your e-mail from here?"

Charlotte nodded. "Already there. Let me just get into the SexyTarot files, so I can get his address… oh, no!"

"What?"

"It's not there. All the accounts have been erased! Could Lou have done that?"

EJ shook his head, smirking. "No, it was more likely Sarah's work. She was probably protecting the accounts from any other illegal access. Let me call her to get the address. She'll have it on hand."

Just a few minutes later, Charlotte had the e-mail

address. EJ continued to talk with his colleagues, apprising them of their plan. Charlotte could tell from the tone of EJ's responses that someone on the other end wasn't exactly a huge fan of what they were doing, but she could also see EJ wasn't about to budge.

It felt strange, sitting here and using Jennie Snow's computer. The faint, spicy fragrance of the woman's perfume still hung in the air, and Charlotte tried to work up a little ire, but couldn't. Jennie had been way too friendly and helpful for Charlotte to feel jealous for long.

Charlotte tended to form quick first impressions, and she'd liked Jennie a lot, even though it was clear the woman had shared an intimate relationship with EJ. Jennie was a supermodel in computer geek's clothing, with her sensuous figure, large brown eyes and long, sleek brunette hair. Charlotte felt totally unglamorous by comparison. And Jennie also worked in the same field as EJ—that gave them a lot in common, so it wasn't much of a surprise that they would have been attracted to each other.

Of course, EJ had gone out of his way to show Charlotte that they had a professional relationship only now. But there was also something haunting about Jennie, something hidden below her smile that Charlotte knew had nothing to do with EJ, and she wondered what it was, though it appeared EJ was not about to say one more word on the issue. She looked at the blank e-mail screen.

"What should I say?" she asked as EJ set his cell phone on the desk.

"Not too much. Just that you want to talk to him, and ask for an online meeting."

She typed in the sparse message, and sent it.

"Well, here's hoping he sees it, or that he agrees to meet." She thought for a moment. "What if he doesn't? Agree, that is? What do we do then?"

EJ shook his head. "I don't know. Try to get you somewhere safe while the investigation continues, I guess."

"I would have to go into hiding?"

"These people mean business, Charlotte. We have to keep you out of their reach."

"So we would go back to Norfolk? Talk to the cops?" Though she spoke hopefully, she sensed that was not what EJ meant at all.

"That could be part of it, though I'd prefer to work through federal agencies, if we can. I'm still not comfortable with how those shooters appeared at Ronny's house right after I'd called for someone to come to that location. The mob often has a few cops in their pocket—though that's not definitely the case here, I want to be careful. We might be able to set something up through DOJ, or the FBI, and put you in a government safe house, which would make me feel better."

"I don't know, EJ. Isn't there something else we could do? My entire life has already been turned upside-down by this, and I am not going to go hide in some government compound when it could take forever to work this out. And what about Ronny?"

EJ wrapped his fingers around the back of her chair, squeezing tightly. He was getting sick and tired of worrying about Ronny, and he honestly couldn't give a rat's ass what happened to the jerk, except insofar as how it affected Charlotte. Couldn't she see what a bad apple her brother was?

"Let's just take one thing at a time. Let's go to the cafeteria here, and we'll come back up in a while to see if Lou has gotten your message."

"I'm not terribly hungry."

He slid his arm around her shoulders, and she felt better—the public sign of closeness made her heart skip a beat, and she snuggled next to him, just slightly.

"Well, they'll only have cafeteria food—it's not the Isle." He laughed, landing a light kiss on her hair and making her heart sing. "But you should eat something. Who knows what the rest of the day holds?"

Charlotte wasn't sure what was going to happen with Lou, but as they moved through the door, EJ gently directing her forward with his hand on the small of her back, she was happy enough right now.

11

CHARLOTTE'S HANDS WERE ICE-COLD as she sat in Jennie's chair, and even EJ's presence as he stood behind her, his hands on her shoulders, didn't do much to comfort her. She was about to sit down and talk with the man who might have hurt her brother, and who was trying to hurt her. The thought filled her with a sense of purpose—she could talk some sense into Lou, she knew she could.

"Just relax, darlin'. He can't hurt you here, and he can't find you on this machine. So just talk, and find out as much as you can, okay?"

Charlotte nodded, and took a deep breath, logging in to the SexyTarot Web page. But no one was there. Lou had not signed in.

"Check your e-mail again."

Sure enough, there was a note. Short and to the point.

Charlotte's heart moved up into her throat, and a little squeak escaped her lips as she read the email from Lou out loud.

"We have your brother. If you want him to stay

alive, come to this address…" She read the address, which EJ realized was in a relatively isolated area outside of D.C., but there was no way Charlotte was going anywhere.

"Unbelievable. He says he wants justice? Is he insane?" Charlotte's voice shook with anger.

"It's mob justice, Charlotte. Not real justice. And yes, it is insane."

"He is a horrible person. I can't believe I discussed his love life with him." She shuddered, wrapping her arms around herself. "Are they going to kill Ronny?"

"If they haven't killed him already, I have to wonder why. It could be a ruse, another way to try to get you, so that they can bait him. Or maybe Ronny has fingered you as the thief, and they're using him to lure you in."

"Ronny wouldn't do that."

Jennie had been silent to this point. Her voice was gentle, but her eyes hard as she spoke. "Sometimes family can turn on you, Charlotte. It's not pretty, but it's true."

"There's no way you can meet him." EJ took a deep breath.

"But I have to! He said—"

"Yeah, well, I'm not giving a gangster the upper hand. We'll work out a plan." EJ's tone brooked no argument, and he looked at Jennie pointedly. "Do you have any information on this location?"

She smiled. "I can do better than that. Let me get a live satellite image, and let's see what we can see."

"You have a satellite watching his house?" Charlotte was amazed enough to forget her fear for a moment.

"No, not just his house, any house. Anyone can link up to Web sites and see satellite images of just about anything they want to see, but what we have access to is just a little more detailed, and up-to-the-minute."

"Scary, Big-Brother stuff."

"Or comforting, keep-us-safe-stuff." Jennie said firmly.

"I guess." Charlotte didn't sound convinced, but EJ was glad to have the resources they did, and watched closely as Jennie pulled the images up on the computers.

The house looked normal enough. A few cars parked outside, and…oh, yeah. Zooming into a close view, it wasn't a perfectly clear image, but clear enough to see several men standing around the property holding some serious firepower.

"Can you print this and overlay the area maps so we can study approaches?"

"Easy as pie."

There was silence in the office for a few minutes, only the sound of the printer pushing out the maps, and EJ was surprised when Jennie spoke.

"Charlotte, would you mind if I spoke to EJ alone for a moment?"

Looking suspicious, Charlotte didn't budge. EJ almost grinned.

"I think I might have an idea, but it requires me

sharing some information that I can only tell some-one with proper clearance. It'll only take a minute."

Charlotte nodded stiffly, obviously miffed, but not wanting to show it. "Fine. I'll take a walk to the ladies' room. Slowly."

"WHAT ARE YOU THINKING, JEN?"

"This isn't going to go away. You know if she goes there she's dead."

EJ inhaled deeply. "I know. I just can't…she doesn't deserve this. It was her brother all the way, not that I want Maloso to hurt him, either. Ronny belongs in jail, not in the river. But there has to be a way around this. Since we know where they are, we can maybe…"

"Do you think he would have given you that ad-dress if he didn't expect you to try to raid? He probably has the guy somewhere else, or he's already dead. I doubt Lou is at the house. This is some kind of trap."

"So what do we do?"

Jennie looked toward the door where Charlotte had stalked out, and smiled. "She's different. I can see it in your eyes."

"How so?" EJ knew he sounded defensive, though he couldn't seem to squelch it.

"She is more than…we were. Maybe more than what you have had with any other woman."

EJ assessed the situation quickly—Jennie didn't appear hurt or angry, just curious. And concerned. Like any friend would be.

"I think so. It's hard to tell under all this stress, but yeah, she's different."

Jennie smiled and put any worries he had about her possessiveness to rest. "I think you can tell more about a relationship when you are under stress than when you aren't. I'm glad for you, *caro*. But are you sure she's not involved? Do you buy her story about Lou? Do you trust her?"

"I do trust her, Jen. I know that's hard for you to understand, coming from the hell you used to live in, but I believe her. She's completely a victim here."

"What have you told her about me? How did you explain how you happened to know me?"

"She guessed we had…something. In the past." He emphasized the phrase, and Jennie just smiled in response. "And I didn't tell her anything about you that would put you in danger—I wouldn't do that, not even with people I trust."

"Thank you. I hope you understand why I had to ask. I needed to know that you trusted her, and what you'd said." Jennie's smile became even warmer, her eyes dancing with amusement. "Oh, you have it bad, EJ, don't you?"

"I refuse to answer that on grounds that it might incriminate me. But yeah, I understand why you had to ask how much she knew. No hard feelings."

They heard Charlotte's footsteps outside in the hallway, and stopped talking for the moment. When she walked back into the office, EJ's heart sank, seeing how miserable she was. She wouldn't look at him.

"Charlotte, are you okay?"

She nodded. Clearly her nose was out of joint regarding Jennie, and the thought almost made him smile. How long had it been since a woman had felt that way about him? Even Millie had always been so comfortable with him, so sure of his affection, that she was never jealous. And his recent girlfriends, well, they knew the score; jealousy didn't figure in when you were just having fun.

He didn't want Charlotte feeling bad, but he had to admit, knowing she was jealous was kind of… nice. He crossed the office to take Jennie's hands in his, a purely platonic contact compared to the hug they'd shared earlier.

"Jen, thanks for all your help. I will definitely put a word in for you with Ian, so expect a phone call."

"I appreciate that, EJ." She leaned in, kissing him quickly, and he smiled when she winked. "Let me keep looking into this before you decide to approach the D.C. house—there could be another way."

"Thanks—I'll contact Ian and we'll stay in touch. Take care."

Jennie walked over to Charlotte, and this time, Charlotte got the hug—EJ smiled at her shocked expression over Jennie's shoulder.

"Be safe, Charlotte. You're in good hands."

Charlotte sputtered, caught between her bad mood and good manners, but manners won out as she offered Jennie a warm smile. "You, too, Jennie. We appreciate your help."

Leaving the office, they were silent as they walked back to the car. Once they were enveloped in the relative safety of the sedan, EJ turned to Charlotte, drew her into his arms, kissing her until neither one of them could breathe evenly. He smiled when Charlotte pulled back, and just said, "Wow."

"Yeah. I didn't want you having any doubts, Charlotte. Jennie is a friend and, who knows, she could end up as part of the unit someday, but for the record, I'm not looking at any other women." He smoothed his hand over her hair, pushing the unruly mass of curls back from her forehead as his gaze wandered tenderly over her face. "How could I? I am so blinded by you. You're the only woman I want to look at, to touch…"

Charlotte didn't say anything, but her emotions were in her eyes, and he had to exert mammoth control to stop from letting go of his own tenuous control right there on the street. He sank back into his seat, starting the car.

"We'd better get going. It's a long drive back."

"We're going back to Norfolk?"

"We need to talk to Ian and Sarah, and see what federal help we can get once we hear back from Jennie. This is big, and we're going to need some big help."

CHARLOTTE LAY in the tub, up to her chin in bubbles, and sighed in perfect contentment. She set her problems aside for the moment to enjoy a bath. They'd driven all the way back to Norfolk, and met in a room where several policemen had questioned her. EJ had left to speak with his partners and a bunch of scary-looking federal agents to come up with a plan, she imagined.

She couldn't remember how long it had been since she'd slept, and time seemed irrelevant in some way. Everything was topsy-turvy, changing from one moment to the next.

She was tired, scared and worried to death about Ronny—no one seemed to think they needed to rush in to save her brother, and tears stung behind her eyes as she realized why. They figured either he was dead, or he was just a criminal. Expendable.

And here she was, safely ensconced in a nice hotel room with EJ, safe for the night with an armed policeman, Officer Thomas, at the door. She wished she could think of something to do, some way to make them move faster, but she was exhausted and had to trust they knew what they were doing.

EJ knew what Ronny meant to her. He wouldn't let him die if he could help it.

As she let the hot water soothe her tense muscles, she was thankful for the fresh clothes Grace had lent her. But that thought made her think of the ruined evening dress. Her beautiful, ruined, shredded dress. It was the least of her problems, but it stood out in her mind as an emblem of everything that had gone wrong. Unrepairable. She'd make it up to Phoebe somehow, she swore to herself. Hopefully the clerk hadn't already lost her job.

As guilt and all the worry about her messed-up life and her brother started to swallow her again, she pushed it back, and made herself relax. For the moment, she was okay. She couldn't help Ronny if she was a mess, so she had to hold it together. She was going to rest, and think of a plan. She would get her life back together, and make it even better than before, for both of them.

EJ had become very noncommittal since they left the police station. Something was up, but she was reluctant to push. She didn't even know what to push for. She didn't know if they had a relationship, or what was between them except sex and danger.

Too exhausted to think one more thought, Charlotte rested her head on the small pillow she'd made out of a folded towel, and scrunched down in the water, blanking her mind of everything except the private mantra she'd been given by a yogi she'd met a few years before.

The next thing she knew, she was dreaming of the softest, most tender kiss she could ever imagine, and smiled into it, resisting her dawning consciousness, wanting to stay wherever it was in her imagination that EJ was kissing her like that—but when she heard his voice, she knew it wasn't in her imagination that the kiss was happening.

"Charlotte, wake up, darlin'. The water's getting cold."

She opened her eyes slowly to see him crouching by the side of the tub, smiling at her. He was so handsome. So amazingly gorgeous inside and out. She had no idea what was in his head, or what exactly his feelings were, and she didn't want to ask for specifics. She just wanted to enjoy what she had with him right now, letting the future take care of itself.

"I fell asleep."

He laughed softly. "Yes, you did. But you're going to get cold soon. Dinner is waiting."

His eyes moved over her hungrily—most of the bubbles had faded, leaving her exposed to his gaze. She didn't mind, and even did a little, sexy stretch for his enjoyment. And when she opened her eyes again and met his hot look, she knew how much he had enjoyed it.

"Let me help you out so you don't slip."

She smiled, letting him take her hand though she had been managing to get out of tubs alone just fine for years. As she rose from the water, she did feel a chill, goose bumps traveling the course of her skin, and her nipples puckered—though that might not have been due to the chill.

"What did you get for dinner?" She tried to sound casual and light, though the way he was looking at her made *her* feel like dinner.

"Uh, just some cheeseburgers and fries, soda—I know you don't eat too much meat, but I thought we needed something with some substance to it. Protein."

"Burgers are fine. Thank you. I'm starving."

She lifted her leg to step over the edge of the tub, and he caught it, fitting his hand into the wet crook behind her knee and sliding it up to cup her bottom. She lowered her foot back to the porcelain, her cool skin burning where he touched.

"Why don't you join me for a quick, hot shower? I'm feeling a little chilled," she said.

He took his hands away from her long enough to quickly undress, grab a condom from the vanity case, and then stepped into the tub with her, sliding the plastic door shut.

"Can't have you getting cold," he teased.

"What about dinner?" she asked.

"I'll go back and get more, later."

As she turned the shower on full, steam filled the stall in seconds, and EJ's hands slid around her waist and planted themselves on the cheeks of her back-side, kneading her while he stroked her tongue with his. He nudged the rock-hard evidence of his excite-ment against her belly, letting her know he was more than ready. Amazingly, so was she, but this all felt so good, she wanted to make it last. She wanted him at her mercy. Seducing him on the sofa had only been the start of the creative loving she hoped to explore with this man.

"Still cold?"

She loved how his voice changed when he was really turned on, how his accent thickened into a heavy drawl and his naturally smooth tone turned rough. "No, baby, I'm heating up quite nicely, thank you."

It was the first time she'd used that kind of endearment with a man, and it thrilled her to her toes. She slid her hands down and stroked him, rubbing her thumb over the slick head of his cock and gloried in the shudder that racked him.

"Charlotte, I want your hands on me, your legs around me…"

He kissed his way down to her shoulder, then slid his hands forward, massaging her breasts as his tongue made a long, slow journey down her torso and nestled in between her legs. She used one hand to part herself for him, and another to steady herself as he plundered, bringing her to the edge too many times to count, but never letting her cross over the threshold. She was shaking when he stood, pressing up close and taking her mouth in a hot kiss all the hotter because of her taste on his lips.

"Wrap your legs around me, Charlotte."

She stopped cold. She was standing up—what was he asking?

"Huh?" Okay, not the sexiest of replies, but she was truly confused.

"I want to lift you up and get inside you. I need you to wrap your legs around and hold on."

"EJ," she started sputtering, losing the mood. "I…I can't. I can't do that."

"Why not?"

She could feel the heat in her face that had nothing to do with the shower.

"I'm not exactly a waif, if you haven't noticed. You can't hold my weight for that long."

Damn him—here she was feeling as embarrassed as she'd ever felt and he…laughed. She drew back in indignation, but he stepped forward with a gleam in his eye that told her he wasn't taking no for an answer.

"Charlotte, you are not heavy, you are perfect. Full and sensual and with curves that make men sweat just looking at you. Believe me, this won't be a problem."

"I don't think…"

"Yes, good, don't think."

The next thing she knew he had backed her against the shower wall, and it was a good thing, she thought, that it was a sturdy wall, because he'd slipped his hands down to her hips and lifted her in one, deft movement. Reflexively, she reached around and held on with arms and legs, feeling him fill her at the very same moment.

Oh, my God. She was having sex, standing up, with a man holding her against a shower stall wall. She'd always been too afraid to fantasize about this particular position, thinking no guy would want to risk damaging his lumbar muscles, but now that she was doing it, and EJ seemed to be having no particular problems keeping her there, she relaxed.

"That's it, darlin', see how good this is?"

"Mmm-hmm."

She experimented, not holding on so much for dear life with her arms, but loosening them to touch him, and following his sensual guidance so that he could move as he needed to, entering her so deeply and touching every part of her so completely that she cried out in surprise as her body wrenched in pleasure, bucking against him as she came.

"Charlotte…"

EJ couldn't say more than her name as he gave in to his own explosion of pleasure, chanting her name, and sinking his fingers into her flesh as he pressed her into the wall, holding her up and pursuing his orgasm with such power that it triggered another lingering one for her.

When they were done, she didn't know if she should laugh or cry, or just thank the heavens.

"EJ."

His face was buried in her neck, his chest heaving, and he didn't respond.

"Uh, EJ?"

"What, darlin'?"

"You can let me down now if you want. The water's getting cold again."

"So it is." He stepped back, holding her as she loosened her legs and tested if her knees still worked. Thinking of how amazing she felt, watching his powerful body flex and bend as he turned to shut off the water, how his lean form and sculpted muscles moved, she found herself becoming choked up.

"Charlotte?" EJ pulled the plastic door back, and reached for a towel, looking back at her. "What's wrong? Did something hurt? Damn, I'm sorry, I wanted that to be good for you...."

Then she laughed, because if he thought that wasn't good for her, he had to be unconscious.

"EJ, I'm fine. I'm better than fine. It's just that you...what we did...how we are...."

Oh, crap, she thought. She was going to burst into tears. She'd heard of that happening sometimes when the sex was powerful, but this didn't have to do with orgasms—it was completely emotional.

"What? Darlin', what?" He helped her out of the shower, wrapping a huge white towel around her, and drawing her into his arms.

"It's just that, I know this sounds stupid but—"

"Just say it, Charlotte. Nothing sounds stupid. You can tell me anything, okay?"

He tipped her head back and she felt calmed, looking so deeply into his concerned eyes.

"You make me feel so…good. You look at me and I feel like my insides turn to melted butter, and what you did just now, I…I've never felt like that. Never had anyone make me feel so desired. So pretty, and well," she laughed, hiccupping and making him smile though she felt silly saying it out loud, "so light."

He drew her into a tight hug, chuckling softly. "Charlotte, you are all that and more. I can't get enough of you."

"Me, either. Of you, I mean."

"Thank God, darlin', because come what may, I don't plan on leaving you anytime soon."

THEY ATE COLD CHEESEBURGERS and fries like it was the nectar of the gods, talked about nothing in particular, and then EJ faced the inevitable and filled her in on the plan. Charlotte snuggled up against him, wrapped in a sheet and nothing else, testing his concentration.

"Will you go with me? To this safe house?"

EJ wrapped his arms around her, holding her as close as physical space allowed.

"I have to be in on the raid—I want to see with my own eyes that he's caught and unable to get at you. But you'll be in the best of hands, completely under heavy guard. We think we have a decent idea of where Maloso is—Jennie made some contacts and has run some new maps." He looked at his watch. "They are supposed to send copies over here soon."

EJ inhaled the freshly washed scent of her hair, the well-loved muskiness of her naked body next to his, and swore on his own grave that he wouldn't let anyone lay one finger on her, ever.

"I can't bear the thought of you getting hurt, EJ. I can't stand to even think of it."

"Same back atcha. Which is why the best place for you is the safe house, until we have Maloso behind bars."

She turned her face upwards to his, lifting her hand to his cheek.

"I mean it. I couldn't stand it if you got hurt protecting me."

"It's my job, sweetheart. But I don't plan on getting hurt. With any luck, we can put this to bed with a minimum of bloodshed."

She burrowed against him. He said reassuringly, "We're going to get through this, Charlotte. Things are going to be okay, and you have to believe that."

"I do, EJ."

She yawned, nestling against him, and feeling his heartbeat steady with his breathing as he fell asleep. She heard a strange noise, and perked up, realizing it was EJ's laptop. Sliding softly out of bed, she walked to the machine, and watched the bar across the center measuring the progress of the files being sent—this had to be the maps from Jennie.

She turned, opening her mouth to wake him, and then changed her mind, staring at the computer until it was finished. Her plan was not so much a plan as a spontaneous reaction, but this was her only chance to do things her way, and try to help her brother.

Reaching for the computer, she opened the down-loaded files, and studied them closely—she didn't know the area, but she wrote down the information, and held her breath, looking back toward where EJ was still sleeping soundly.

Slipping the clothes she'd laid out over her head, she then grabbed her purse. She had to get by the guard. She'd try to claim female problems or some-thing similar, that she needed a trip to the drugstore. Men were typically so uncomfortable with those things, and with any luck Officer Thomas was no ex-ception.

Opening the door, she peered outside and stopped short, gasping but unable to scream as a hand clamped hard over her mouth. Officer Thomas wasn't a problem—and he wasn't any help, either. He was unconscious…or dead. Shot, he slumped against the wall at a sick angle, blood covering one side of his chest, and Charlotte started to fight against her captor, biting and kicking to free herself and yell for EJ, who was just yards away, but then something hard hit her and everything became dark.

12

"THE HOUSE IS ABOUT twenty miles outside of the city, in a wooded area next to the Dismal Swamp. He's probably got her there. And maybe the brother, too," Ian said.

"If he hurts her, I'll kill him myself," EJ swore.

"We'll get her, EJ."

Ian drove the point home as EJ sat at the desk, his mind sifting through every detail of the plan for the thousandth time.

"I never would have pinned Thomas as the leak," Ian said.

"I wish they hadn't killed him—I would have liked my shot at him."

"You've got to get your head on straight, my friend. You won't be any help to her like this. How the hell did she end up outside that room anyway?" Ian asked.

EJ shrugged, castigating himself endlessly for falling asleep. He hadn't heard anything, but had awakened hours later to find the body in the hall and Charlotte gone. If anything happened to her, it would be his fault for letting his guard down.

"I would have heard if someone knocked. They had to have lured her outside somehow," EJ said.

"Or she was trying to get out—maybe she is on the inside of this thing," Ian said pointedly.

EJ looked at Ian in surprise, and nearly lost it. "That's crossing the line, Ian. She's not in on this. I'd bet my life on it."

"Well, that's pretty much exactly what you're doing—and several other lives as well."

"If she was trying to get out of that room, it was probably because she wanted to save that brother of hers again. I know she's been upset that we haven't been concentrating on that."

"You think she was going to try to go after him herself?" Ian asked.

"Who the hell knows? It wouldn't have been the first time."

Ian slanted him a look. "This is going to be a tough situation, so stay cool."

"Oh, I'm downright chilly."

"I was thinking the opposite." Ian pinned him with a look that saw to the heart of the matter. "You're in love with her."

"I don't know if I would go that far. I care about her."

Ian laughed, shaking his head. "I seem to recall, not so long ago, our positions were reversed, and you were making me face facts about Sage. We had a few tense moments back then, and that was mostly because I was being an ass. But I've been where you are, bud. In a tense situation and not wanting to see the woman you…*care about*…in danger. It can push you into making bad decisions."

EJ remembered all too well when their team had just been forming, and Ian and Sage were struggling through their own troubles. Ian had called in EJ and Sarah to help, then changed their well-orchestrated plan to take off on his own.

Ian's rash decision to take on the situation alone, to spare Sage any more conflict, had ended up putting her in even more danger. Sage had been shot, though thankfully the wound hadn't been fatal, but Ian hadn't let himself off the hook for that for a long time. If ever.

EJ simply couldn't let himself so much as think of anything happening to Charlotte. "I hear you loud and clear, Ian. I'll stick to the plan. But if I find her hurt, or worse—" he could barely say the word, "—all bets are off."

"EJ…"

EJ met and held his friend's eyes, his voice raw. "She might be pregnant, Ian. She might be carrying my baby."

Nothing he could have said would have shocked his friend more, and what should have been a happy moment between them just raised the sense of urgency.

"You know that?"

"No, it's just a possibility. We, uh, got carried away. Once."

"Unlike you, my friend, to get carried away. But I think maybe it's about time."

"You can get all misty-eyed on me later, Ian. Time's short."

Ian looked outside the glass window where Sarah stood dressed in black night-gear from head to toe with a group of S.W.A.T. guys and federal agents. Everyone wanted in on this job; Maloso would be a big prize, but Ian was more worried about EJ, and now, about Charlotte. Thinking of Sage at home, very pregnant with their daughters, stiffened his resolve to end this soon, and well.

"Then let's go get her."

CHARLOTTE WISHED for the one millionth time that she never stepped foot outside that hotel room, as she sat tied and bound to a chair in the middle of the garage of what seemed to be a standard issue development house. Nothing stood out that she could use to identify where she was, and she'd been unconscious until just a short while ago.

Her head hurt, her heart hurt, and when she moved her jaw, something very unpleasant popped and shot pain up to her eye. So she kept her mouth shut.

In the end, all she could really be grateful for was that if the men who had grabbed her in the hallway had stormed into their room, they could have killed EJ before taking her. It was her only serious comfort to know that hadn't happened. And she knew, in her heart, that EJ wouldn't stop looking until he found her.

She hoped that was sooner than later.

There was the sound of a key in a door, and some men walked into the garage. They were well-dressed, casual but expensive, as if they were going out to play golf at an expensive resort. One man in particular watched her with sharp black eyes.

"So you are Charley, my little psychic."

She met his stare. "You must be Lou, my little mob guy."

The men laughed and Lou nodded. "You have guts, I'll give you that."

"Where's my brother?"

"You mean the other lying son of a bitch who stole from me? Don't worry, he's still around. I wanted to have you two thieves in the same place, so I could watch you both die. Family is important, after all."

Charlotte spit on the floor. "You are the son of a bitch, Lou. And you kill people, you steal from people, you sell drugs…"

"Whoa! I have never sold drugs. Ask my buddies here—Giacco, have I ever sold drugs?"

A big man by the door shook his head in all seriousness. "No way, Lou. Dirty things, drugs. Dirty money."

Lou nodded. "That's right. Technology, and working the stocks, that's more my gig."

Charlotte tipped her chin up. "You want to hurt

me, hurt my brother. All he did was take some money, and we could give it back. You don't need to hurt us."

Lou stared at her for a moment, and she was sure she could see that he was empty inside—there was nothing there but cold emptiness.

"You don't tell me my business, lady. You screw me over, I screw you over harder. That's how it goes. That's *business*."

She tried a different tack. "You don't have to do it that way, Lou. You end up just hurting yourself more in the end."

"Really? And how's that?"

"You build up bad karma—it will catch up to you, you know," she said.

"What goes around comes around is what you're saying?"

"Yes."

"Then I guess you could see me making things even with you and your brother as the same thing, right?"

"Good one, Lou." Giacco nodded heavily.

"Shut up, Giacco. What the hell do you know?"

Lou turned back to Charlotte, giving her an evil smile.

"Anyway, you want to see your brother? Fine. We can arrange that."

Charlotte didn't say a word, but felt like she would burst from the chair, worried and elated all at the same time that either they meant to take her wherever Ronny was—which could be a bad thing—or that the police were wrong and Ronny was not dead already, at all.

Three seconds later she breathed a gusty sigh of mixed horror and relief when two men dragged Ronny through the garage door, his face bruised almost beyond recognition, and he couldn't step on one leg. His hands were bound, and they shoved him roughly to the floor at her feet, his face hitting the painted cement with a sickening thud.

"Oh, God. Ronny!"

Charlotte strained against her bonds, wanting to lift her brother from the floor, but she was tied too tightly. Ronny groaned, lifting his face up, and glared at Maloso.

"I told you, she had nothing to do with it. It was my game."

"Yeah, and I was born yesterday." Lou nodded to Giacco and the big man walked over, giving Ronny a solid kick in the ribs, and Charlotte screamed, begging them to stop.

Lou walked up to her, so close she could smell the overdose of aftershave he wore, and she almost gagged as he pinched her chin hard between his fingers and lifted her face to his.

"You worried, lady? You should be."

She shook her face loose of his grasp, feeling desperate. "What do you want from us? Tell me, just don't hurt him anymore!"

Lou made clucking sounds. "Oh, sorry. No go. You want to play in the big leagues, you play by our rules. But don't worry—" he dragged a finger down the line of her chin "—I don't plan on hitting your brother any more right now. Because I know that the best way to hurt him now, is to hurt you."

He drew his hand back and Charlotte braced herself for the pain but it didn't come. Someone was calling Lou's name, staying the swing of his powerful arm.

"Boss, there's a problem. You need to come in here."

"This can't wait? You see I'm busy here?"

"It's the New Jersey deal. Things are going bad. They want you on the phone now."

"Jesus, when it rains it pours! All right!"

He looked down in disgust at Charlotte and Ronny, and Charlotte let her breath go, grateful beyond words that the New Jersey deal was going bad.

"Looks like you two can have a little quality time together. But don't worry, this won't take long."

The men all filed into the house, glaring at Charlotte and Ronny in turn, and then the door closed behind them and they were alone.

"I told you to get out of town, Charlotte—how'd they get to you?"

"Long story. Ronny, how could you do this? How could you have gotten involved in something like this? And dragged me into it as well!"

Through his bruises, he met her eyes, shocked at her temper. "I was doing it for us. I wanted to stash enough money away so that you wouldn't have to work those stupid jobs anymore, and we could live right."

"You're trying to tell me you did this *for me?*"

"Well, sure."

Anger beyond words gripped her, and she didn't have the words to tell him what she thought of his plan, but if they lived through this, he was going to get an earful.

But then she saw something that made her love him all over again. He was wiggling his hands loose.

"Ronny, how…?"

"I've been messing with this tape all afternoon, finally stretched it out enough so I could still look like I was tied up, but loose enough to get free so I could make my move when I had the chance."

"Ronny, I love you."

He grinned, scooting behind her chair and pulling at her bindings until she was able to help and within a minute, was free herself. Hope blossomed, and she fell to her knees, wrapping her arms around him in a tight hug.

"I thought you were dead." Sobs choked her, and he hugged her back, but then pulled her up to her feet, closing his eyes with pain as he stood.

"I'm not yet, but we will be if we don't get outta here…"

"Yes, right. But where will we go?" she asked.

"It's pitch-black out—if we can get away from the house into the woods, make it to the edge of the swamp, I don't know, maybe we can flag someone down for help in the morning," he suggested.

"Anything is better than standing here. Let's go."

Miraculously, there was only one guy outside the house, and he stood a good distance away, closer to the front door. Luck was on their side again.

"This way." Ronny had to lean on her, and it was slow progress to the edge of the woods, but once they were in the trees, he picked up a large stick from the ground to lean on, and they made better time.

Better time to where, exactly, she had no idea, but as far away as they could get from Lou was the best direction she could imagine. She'd heard about this area, and that there was a good deal of wildlife—including black bears and bobcats—but better to deal with the animals out here than the ones back at Maloso's house, she thought.

"There have to be some other buildings around here, people—it's a wildlife refuge, isn't it?"

"Yeah, but we have no idea where we are."

Charlotte signaled him to stop for a moment, trying to think about the rough direction they'd taken from the road, and closed her eyes tight, trying to re-imagine the map she'd seen on EJ's computer.

Her concentration was broken by the sound of yelling and a gunshot. Then there were more gunshots.

"They know we're gone, c'mon!"

"No, wait." She listened, and there was a strange sound, like firecrackers, something bursting, and then some more gunshots. "Why would there be so much shooting just because we're gone? Who are they shooting at, each other?"

"I don't really care who they're shooting at, let's just get the hell out of here."

She turned to him, hardly able to see anything but the outline of his shoulders in the dark. The sliver of moon offered some light, but barely.

"No, don't you see? It's the police! They found me!"

"Why would the cops find you?"

"So much has happened, Ronny, I can't explain it all now, but we have to head back toward the house. If we bear more to the right, we should come out at the road, and have enough distance to see—"

"No way. If it is the police, I'm certainly not walking back and letting them get me—I just got free from these guys! C'mon."

He grabbed her arm but she pulled away, confused at his response, but adamant that they needed to go back. She had to make him listen.

"Ronny, I know them. I know one of them, one of the police. He's…just trust me. He'll help us. You don't have to be afraid."

Ronny was silent, staring at her in the darkness, and she heard him sigh in disgust. "Did you go and get yourself involved with a cop, little sister? Damn…"

"I'm your *big* sister, Ronny, and well, yeah. He's

a good man. He's been keeping me safe from the mess *you* got me into. They were investigating me because of you—they thought I was guilty of the thefts. How could you do that to me?"

"We're back to that again? Do you really want to have this conversation here, right now? Are you crazy? I told you, I was trying to do a good thing," he said sullenly.

"Right, okay. But it didn't work out that way, did it? And now we need help. EJ'll help us. Come back with me, Ronny. It'll be okay," she pleaded.

"I'm not goin' anywhere, and you aren't, either! I'm not going to get blown into the cops by my own sister!"

She stood frozen in the darkness, disbelieving what she was hearing. What would he do? Drag her along? Just like Lou's men did?

"Ronny, I love you, but I'm sorry, I'm not going with you."

"Fine, have it your way, but I'm outta here, and don't you dare—"

He was cut off when he hit the ground with a solid thud as she grabbed the walking stick and jerked it away. Charlotte winced, tears stinging her eyes, but she wiped them away. She was going to do what was best for Ronny, and for herself, even if it hurt him now, it might save him later.

"What the hell? Ow!" He struggled to stand, searching the ground for another source of support, but found nothing, his bad leg collapsing beneath him as he fell again on the uneven turf.

His voice was loud, belligerent. "You'd do this to me? To your own brother?"

"What about what you did to me? Doesn't that count?"

"I had good intentions, I wanted a better life for us. You are just going to leave me here crippled in the woods so you can go snuggle up with your cop after you help him arrest me!"

Charlotte shook her head, regret and pain choking her. In the darkness of the woods, she saw now what she never managed to see before in the clear light of day, because she'd wanted family of her own so badly. So much she'd given up her own self-respect to have it. Maybe she couldn't see her brother's self-ishness sooner, but she was getting a good dose of it now, and thanks to EJ, she had the confidence to deal with it.

"I still love you, Ronny, but I don't have to put up with this. You did a bad thing, and you have to take responsibility for it."

She turned away, leaving him alternately cursing and begging as she started walking back toward the house. As she got closer, she could see lights flashing through the trees, and there was a massive crunching of footsteps through the forest. Her face ached where she'd been hit, her eyes were blurred with tears, and branches swiped her bare arms as she marched forward. They would find her, and Ronny, in a minute, so she just kept walking toward the light.

EJ WAS GOING out of his mind. Where was she? They'd stormed the place with everything they had, and the surprise had been to their advantage. But while Lou Maloso and his goons were already on their way to a federal holding tank, there was no sign of Charlotte or her brother, save the bloodied and broken bonds they'd found in the garage. His stomach lurched to think that blood might be Charlotte's.

They'd been there for an hour already, and the search teams were heading into the woods. They'd be bringing in dogs soon. That was never good. Everything was in chaos as agents and cops from everywhere crawled all over the house and grounds like ants, ambulances appearing out of nowhere with sirens screaming, and the media was sure not to be far behind.

But his thoughts were only on Charlotte. He wanted to go out and plow through the trees himself, but it was better to stay out of the way and leave the professionals to it—he would wait here, wait for her to come back. He didn't plan on moving from this spot until he knew something, though he was afraid of what he might come to know. More afraid than he had been, ever, of anything.

He didn't realize he hadn't moved a muscle in several minutes until Sarah and Ian approached him, concern written plainly on their faces, their tones trying to bolster him.

"Hey, man, this was good work. Put away some major figures and with the evidence they're turning up in that house, none of the guys are going to see the light of day anytime soon, especially Lou Maloso."

Sarah kicked at the dirt. "Not to bring up a sore subject, but won't his, uh, associates, be looking to even the score? If…when we do find Charlotte, shouldn't she go into witness protection?"

Ian shook his head. "Typically, no. EJ's friend Jennie seems to think we got the remaining core of Maloso's men here, and the other stragglers will find work with other bosses, who are always anxious to take over new territory. They could care less if Maloso is out of the way. Though she can have witness protection if she wants it."

"But we can't find Charlotte." It was all EJ said, looking toward the woods, and Ian and Sarah exchanged worried looks, also afraid of what the final news might be, but then shouts went up, and lights flashed on out in the woods.

Heart in his throat, EJ walked toward the spot where all the commotion gathered.

And he saw her. Her face was bruised, tear-stained and pale, but she was walking on her own with a search crew officer on either side of her, and when she raised her eyes to meet his, he started breathing again.

"Charlotte."

He stepped forward, tightly gathering her up to him. The men around them backed off. Ian and Sarah stood on the sidelines, grinning like fools.

"Charlotte." It was all he could do, to hold her and say her name, reassuring himself that she was really there, alive and whole.

His.

"Oh, EJ. I knew it was you, I told Ronny, but he wouldn't come…" Her voice was trembling, but it was the most beautiful sound he'd ever heard. EJ loosened his hold a little to look down into her face.

"Ronny is alive? He's out there?"

She nodded, her eyes so sad he couldn't bear it.

"He just wanted to escape, but he'd h-hurt his leg and couldn't walk…I took away his walking stick, and he fell. He wouldn't come back to face up to what he did, but I think they'll find him any minute now. He couldn't have g-gone t-too far. I told him you'd help, but he wouldn't come back with me, so I left him th-there…"

"Oh, baby, I'm so sorry you had to go through this."

"It's okay. I'm okay. I mean, I'm sad about Ronny, but this is for the best for him, too, I think. He doesn't think so now, but maybe later, he'll see…"

EJ made soothing sounds, reassuring her that he was sure that was all true as he walked her back toward the front yard of the house, where an ambulance had been parked since they got there. Handing her over gently to the medics who helped her up into the ambulance, he looked back over his shoulder to see that she was exactly right. The search team had reemerged from the woods with a beaten and lame Ronny in tow.

Charlotte was inside the ambulance, and couldn't see, but he smiled at her, patting her arm.

"Wait one second, darlin'. I have to see to something."

He stepped back to the ground, walking toward Ronny, intercepting him before they made it to the ambulance. He looked at the officers on either side of Ronny who held him up, and nodded.

"Ronny Fulsom?"

The bruised man looked up, worn down and exhausted, but EJ couldn't find it in himself to really feel sorry for the man. Not after what he'd put his sister through.

"I'm Detective Ethan Beaumont."

"Yeah, what? You the cop who's messing with my sister?"

If the man hadn't been so beaten, EJ would have been tempted to do it himself, but he clenched his fists, and managed a dangerous smile.

"You should know I've become rather fond of your sister, and I'm damned sure she doesn't deserve what's happened to her all because of you." EJ stepped a little closer, lowering his voice, and the smile vanished.

"If you weren't already broken to bits, I would be happy to do the job myself. But seeing as you are, regretfully, probably going to end up as my brother-in-law, and Charlotte, being the soft-hearted person that she is, still hopes that you can be a real brother to her someday, I guess I'll have to settle for just arresting you. But let me tell you this…"

He took one step closer, nose-to-nose with Ronny's bloodied face, the other man's eyes wide. EJ felt Ian's hand on his shoulder, warning, and he shook it off. He was perfectly in control.

"If you ever cause your sister one moment of pain again, I will make sure to return it tenfold. No doubt your sister will have some kind word to say, or maybe you can testify against Maloso, something that may end up softening your sentence a bit, but if you ever treat her badly again, you'll deal with me, and that will make your time with Lou look like a walk in the park. Are we clear?"

Underneath the dirt and grime, Ronny paled and lowered his eyes, and EJ stepped back, letting the officers take him to the ambulance, where the officer on his left continued reading his rights.

EJ turned to head back so that he could ride to the hospital with Charlotte, and ran smack into Ian and Sarah, who stood side-by-side, arms crossed, grinning at him like they'd just won a million bucks. All Sarah said, as she hit him solidly in the chest, was, "So he's going to be your brother-in-law, huh? Interesting addition to the family."

EJ shot her a look and walked past, though he smiled as he closed the distance between him and Charlotte.

13

CHARLOTTE POPPED THE TOP of the canned lemonade and held the coolness against her still-sore cheek. Thankfully her cheekbone had only been badly bruised and not fractured, so she didn't require surgery. But it still hurt quite a bit every time she tried to open her mouth too far. Unless EJ was kissing her; that didn't seem to hurt much at all.

It was still uncertain, whatever was between them. It had only been two days since the confrontation at Lou's, and she'd spent the better part of the day in between asleep with the pills they'd given her for pain. So there hadn't been any talk, though his eyes and kisses spoke volumes. She wondered if that would change after she told him her news. She hadn't been able to get the nerve up to tell him yet.

But she'd woken up this morning, at EJ's home, in his bed—alone—ready to start getting her life back together. He'd taken her there from the hospital, and left a note on the counter that he'd be back later that afternoon—he had a meeting about the arrests.

She needed to find out Ronny's court dates, and get him a lawyer, though a court-appointed attorney was probably the best they were going to do. She hadn't forgiven Ronny, not by a long shot. But he was her brother, her only family, and she was willing to stick by him and help him be the man he could be, if he were willing to try. And if that didn't happen, well, she'd cross that bridge when she came to it, but for now, she at least felt like she was seeing things more realistically.

She stopped on the sidewalk and faced the doorway of the community center thrift shop. It was time to face the music about the dress, but as difficult as this was, Charlotte was glad to finally be able to deal with it. She just hoped Phoebe was still there, and hadn't lost her job. If she had, Charlotte fully intended to speak to the manager and make sure she did her best to get the girl's position reinstated.

Chin up, she walked through the door and headed directly to the desk, hoping to see Phoebe's friendly face there.

Instead, there was an older woman, a cool-looking and much less friendly appearing brunette. It must be Sharon, Phoebe's boss. The woman looked up, meeting Charlotte's gaze.

"May I help you?"

"I—I was looking for Phoebe."

"She's in the back room, just a moment."

Charlotte nearly melted in relief—at least the girl hadn't been fired.

She flipped through some items on the racks, and heard a delighted squeal of welcome as she turned to find Phoebe walking toward her with a big smile. Charlotte found herself wrapped in a huge hug and it made her feel even worse. Phoebe was obviously glad to see her, probably because she expected the dress would finally be returned. She took a deep breath and just said what she had to say.

"Phoebe, I am so sorry about the dress—"

The young woman drew back, and looked at Charlotte in amazement.

"Are you kidding? I mean, I was a little frazzled the morning you didn't show up, but I understand completely and I'm just so happy to see that you're okay!"

"You are?" Now Charlotte was confused.

"Yes, I got the note from Mr. Beaumont, saying you'd had an accident and the dress we'd lent you had been ruined, but he had another identical one that was brand-new sent immediately to replace it."

Charlotte was frozen in shock. EJ had replaced the dress. But he had never said a word…of course, if he had, she would have argued. She preferred to pay her own way, but in the case of the dress, she just breathed a heavy sigh of relief.

"I didn't know—he must have meant to tell me and forgot. You didn't get in trouble? I was so worried."

Phoebe slung an arm around her shoulders and walked with her out the front door where they could stand in the sunshine and chat in private.

"Well, Sharon wasn't thrilled with me loaning the dress out—but she couldn't be too mad because it was replaced, and then some. The new dress went for big dollars in the auction, She chewed me out a little, but that was it."

"Well, I'm sorry that happened. I really was the one who should be chewed out."

"Those are terrible bruises on your face—you must have been in some accident. I'm glad to see you're up and around."

"Oh, thanks. Yeah, today is my first day out. I'm still a little woozy."

Phoebe hugged her again. "Well, you met one amazing guy. He's the one you got the dress for in the first place, to go to the Isle, that's him, right? He's the one who replaced the dress?"

Charlotte smiled. "Yeah, that's him."

"Wow. Sounds like a fairy tale."

Charlotte nodded, thinking about how the original Grimm fairy tales had been scary stories with hard lessons, as well as a happily-ever-after, and while she and EJ had surely experienced the scary and difficult parts, she wondered about the happily-ever-after. And hoped.

"Well, I should be going. I'm sorry again about the dress, but I'm glad it worked out okay."

"You still owe me a tarot reading, remember," Phoebe teased, winking.

"Absolutely. You just say when. You can have as many as you want, whenever you want."

"Cool!"

Waving goodbye to Phoebe, she strolled down the sidewalk, and all she could think about was seeing EJ, and thanking him for replacing that dress.

EJ AND SARAH sat at the long board table with Ian and about a dozen other law enforcement officials going over the arrests and events of the past few days, and all EJ wanted to do was get the hell out of there and go home to Charlotte.

He liked the sound of that, and he wanted to make it a permanent arrangement. He knew when he'd awakened that morning next to her, as she slept peacefully beside him, that she was the woman he wanted to wake up next to for the rest of his life.

Now he couldn't wait to get home and tell her that. He glanced at his watch impatiently as the meeting dragged on, thankfully interrupted by the ring of someone's cell phone, and everyone searched their pockets, but Ian said. "It's me."

EJ knew what the call was as he watched the color run out of his friend's face. Ian clicked the phone shut, stood and declared the meeting over with.

Sage was on her way to the hospital, in labor.

Congratulations and back-slapping went all

around the room, but Ian was already out the door, with EJ and Sarah not far behind.

"Ian, wait, we'll drive."

Racing to the parking garage, the elevator opened and the three of them nearly plowed Charlotte over as they pushed forward. EJ steadied her and pulled her back into the compartment as they headed to the cars.

Ian looked completely shell-shocked, and Sarah was staring at him helplessly, unsure what to do. EJ just laughed out loud, so full of joy at the moment he couldn't keep it inside. Charlotte looked at them all like they were nuts, and he leaned down and kissed her for it.

"Sage is having their twins now. We're going to the hospital," he offered by way of explanation, watching her face light up as she crossed the small space to Ian and hugged him tightly. EJ watched as she placed a palm on either side of his face, as if they were age-old friends, and told him that everything was going to be just fine.

EJ loved her so much he felt like he was going to explode if he didn't tell her, but the doors opened, and they all burst from the elevator, running to the car and directing Ian into the passenger's seat, whether he liked it or not.

When they hit the street, two squad cars were waiting with lights flashing, and they escorted them to the hospital. EJ grinned in the rearview mirror at Charlotte, who sat in back with Sarah, and she grinned back. Within minutes they were at the hospital entrance, and Ian's door was open and he was out almost before EJ had stopped the car. EJ, Sarah and Charlotte went to find parking, and Sarah shook her head.

"I hope those babies waited for him."

"He'll feel much better once he gets up there, one way or the other."

"These are his first, I take it?" Charlotte asked, trying to catch up.

EJ nodded. "Ian was married before and his ex-wife had a bad miscarriage. He's been scared to death on some level that he could lose them again, or lose Sage. I know how he feels, to some extent." He caught her eyes in a meaningful glance in the rearview as he pulled into a space, but she looked away, making him frown.

"Well, let's go see how the new dad is doing."

Finding maternity was a challenge, but eventually they got there, but there was no sign of Ian. A nurse told them everything was fine, but they had just moved on to delivery. It wouldn't be too long now, before they would have news.

Sarah was on her cell to Logan, knowing he would want to be there. For the moment, there wasn't anything they could do but wait. And pace, as was traditional.

But EJ had things to say, and now seemed as good a time as any. He excused them for a moment, leading Charlotte down the hall to an empty room, and asked a nurse if he could use it for a private conversation. The pretty RN was charmed, and agreed.

"EJ! What are you thinking? We have to get back down there, Ian could be back out at any second—"

He stopped her with a kiss that took them both over for several seconds, their emotions running high and their passion for each other spiking to match. EJ drew back, looking down into her face intently, running his finger lightly along the bruises on her cheek.

"I died a thousand deaths when they were looking for you in those woods."

Her face softened, her gaze locked on his. "Me, too. When they took me, I thought I might never see you again."

"I love you, Charlotte. I want to marry you, if you'll have me, as soon as is humanly possible."

"What?" It was all she could think to say, and stood staring dumbly at EJ, who suddenly sank to one knee, and was staring up at her, his heart in his eyes.

"Will you marry me, Charlotte? I should have a ring, and we'll go out to dinner, back to the Isle, and I'll do this again, right, but I can't wait. I need to know now if you'll be my wife."

Charlotte was overcome, and simply sank to her knees, too, grasping his other hand.

"EJ, before I answer that we have to talk about something."

His brow creased in a frown, but he nuzzled her face gently with his lips. "Whatever you want."

Charlotte tried to speak, but the intense emotions of the last few days, hell, the last week, finally caught up with her and she dissolved, leaning into EJ and just sobbing for all she was worth. EJ rubbed her back, his tone apologetic.

"I'm sorry, honey, I've been so impatient. You don't have to answer now. You can take your time, I just want to be part of your life, and have you in mine, we don't have to get married right now if—"

"Nothing happened."

He looked at her blankly, shaking his head.

"What do you mean?"

"When we forgot to be careful? Nothing happened—I'm not pregnant."

EJ drew back, a shocked kind of realization on his face. "You think that's why I'm asking you to marry me?"

Charlotte shook her head in the negative, more tears spilling.

"You replaced the dress!"

It took him a moment to catch up, but then realized what she meant.

"Yes, I know. I knew you were worried about it, and didn't want the clerk to lose her job. I also knew you would argue with me if I told you. I didn't mean to interfere, I love you just the way you are. I was just wanting to…help."

"No, it was a wonderful thing to do. No one has ever done anything so thoughtful for me before. Everything is upside down, and I didn't plan to have a baby, but then I fell so much in love with you, and I started to love the idea of carrying that little baby around, and last night before they could give me pain medication they had to do a test when I told them there was a chance, and then they told me it was negative, and I was s-so…s-sad…and then I found out you replaced that dress, and I was so touched. I needed to see you right away."

The tirade ended in even heavier tears, and EJ pulled her into a tight embrace, rocking her back and forth until she calmed down, kissing her hair and smiling. When the tears had reduced to hiccups, he drew back, studying her face, his voice patient.

"Charlotte, do you love me?"

He kissed her softly.

"Yes."

"Do you want to have babies with me and fill all those empty rooms in my family home? To have a future with me?"

He kissed her again, more deeply, licking the salty tears from her lips.

"Oh, yes."

"Then, please, once more, will you marry me?"

She met him full-on, their passion exploding as they lowered to the floor, laughing against each others' lips as she responded from the deepest well of her heart.

"Absolutely."

Epilogue

Four years later...

"GOD, I LOVE A woman in uniform," Logan whispered to Sage and Charlotte. His eyes were glued to Sarah as she stood at the podium next to Ian and EJ, all impressive and proud in their formal dress uniforms.

Jennie—who'd joined the team shortly after Ian and Sage's daughters were born—stood with them, and Nathan Reilley, next to her, the most recent member of the team. The unit was receiving commendations as a team and individually for the excellent work they'd done for the previous five years.

The Virginia HotWires office was now the model for similar units being formed all over the country. Small, specialized units were being annexed onto police departments and existing computer crime units, blending federal technical expertise with local law enforcement. It was proving to be a winning combination.

"I think Sarah looks a little misty," Sage commented with a broad grin. Her two dark-haired, blue-eyed daughters, Anna and Rose, were quietly fascinated—for the moment—with the sight of their daddy, aunt and uncles up on the stage.

"It's the hormones, but don't say anything." Logan grinned, looking forward to adding his own child to the growing HotWires family. "She vehemently denies any mood changes."

Charlotte chuckled, keeping one finger hooked into the collar of Jared, who was two, and who badly wanted to go up on stage and see what all the fuss was about.

"You did a magnificent job with the flowers, Charlotte—those hydrangeas are unbelievable, and in November!"

"Thanks, Sage—they're from my new collection in the greenhouse. We're so busy I'm going to have to take on more help soon, especially with the new addition on the way."

Logan leaned down to Sage. "You and Ian expanding the team, by any chance?"

"We've been talking about adoption. One more would be nice—a boy, maybe. And we both like the idea of giving a child in need a home."

Logan squeezed her shoulder in support, and returned his eyes to the stage. The ceremony was over, and congratulations were offered all around, flashes from cameras coming from every direction.

"I'm so glad that part's over, I could eat a moose.

How long before the dinner?" Sarah joined the group first, blushing as Logan pulled her into a deep hug, and missing the humorous looks exchanged by her friends and partners. A beeping sound had everyone checking their pockets, but Sage popped up.

"It's mine. Sorry guys, keeping an eye on a contract we're trying to get in D.C."

Kissing Ian apologetically, but with a sensual promise in her eyes, she turned away to take the call, and Ian's two girls flew into his arms, nearly toppling him over.

Grace laughed, her eyes on Nathan—the sexy new team member and the youngest of the group—as he joined the group. Grace's date, Jordan, stepped up possessively sliding his arm around her as he offered congratulations to Ian and the rest of the group.

Ian's daughter, Rose, spoke at the top of her lungs, wanting to make sure she got her two cents in among all the adult conversation. "Daddy! You look handsome and sexy!"

Ian quirked an eyebrow, wondering where his daughter had come up with that particular description, and peered over at Sage, who winked at him and shrugged. Looking down at the giggling girls he shook his head.

EJ teased, "You are *so* going to have your hands full when those two get older."

Ian looked up, more content than he ever imagined being. "You look like your hands are pretty full now, my friend."

EJ held Jared, who wiggled and pulled at his dad's police hat, and EJ set it on his son's head, obscuring his face completely. Everyone laughed, heading toward the round dinner tables set with pristine white linen cloths, crystal and gleaming silver. Cloth napkins were folded into roses, and expensive sprays of flowers—arranged by Charlotte's recently opened shop—completed the festive decorations.

Jennie ran a finger along the edge of a lily blossom, smiling at Charlotte. "You've outdone yourself, *cara.*"

Free of holding onto Jared, Charlotte basked in the praise and squeezed Jennie's hand in thanks. Jennie had become such a close friend over the years, practically an aunt to Jared, as well as to Ian and Sage's girls, but Charlotte wished Jennie could find happiness with children of her own.

For whatever reason, Jennie shied away from serious relationships, even though Charlotte was sure Nathan was interested. Charlotte knew Jennie had secrets she never spoke of, and Charlotte didn't push. She wondered absently if Nathan would be that polite, though, watching the young man's eyes turn hot as they took in Jennie's sensual beauty. Time would tell.

"How's Ronny doing, Charlotte?" Sarah asked as she picked hungrily from a tray of appetizers. Charlotte grinned and heeded Logan's earlier warning. Sarah was only two months along and still getting used to the idea of her pregnancy. Even though she and Logan had been trying for over a year, the reality was still settling in.

"He's doing pretty well. He's been working on his college degree in youth counseling, course by course, and should be eligible for parole next year."

"That's fabulous. You've done so well standing by him like you have. Not everyone has that kind of family love around them. I can't imagine how he wouldn't make a go of it."

"Well, I had EJ's support. EJ and Ian used their clout to keep him close to home so I could visit, and I think that meant a lot. It hasn't been easy for Ronny, and he still has a way to go, but he's grown a lot."

"That's good to hear."

They all took their places at the head table, settling in as servers in white uniforms began to deliver the first courses, and Ian picked up a crystal flute of champagne, lifting it to his team and their families.

"To new beginnings," he said, his eyes locked on Sage's sparkling gaze.

"To new beginnings," EJ and Sarah chimed in, echoed by all the others as glasses clinked and the celebration went forth.

CB WITHDRAWN ~ms, JB

FREE

2 BOOKS AND A SURPRISE GIFT!

We would like to take this opportunity to thank you for reading this Mills & Boon® book by offering you the chance to take TWO more specially selected titles from the Blaze® series absolutely FREE! We're also making this offer to introduce you to the benefits of the Mills & Boon® Reader Service™—

★ FREE home delivery
★ FREE gifts and competitions
★ FREE monthly Newsletter
★ Books available before they're in the shops
★ Exclusive Reader Service offers

Accepting these FREE books and gift places you under no obligation to buy; you may cancel at any time, even after receiving your free shipment. Simply complete your details below and return the entire page to the address below. You don't even need a stamp!

YES! Please send me 2 free Blaze books and a surprise gift. I understand that unless you hear from me, I will receive 4 superb new titles every month for just £3.10 each, postage and packing free. I am under no obligation to purchase any books and may cancel my subscription at any time. The free books and gift will be mine to keep in any case.

K7ZEE

Ms/Mrs/Miss/Mr...Initials ....
BLOCK CAPITALS PLEASE

Surname ....

Address ....

....

....Postcode ....

Send this whole page to:

The Reader Service, FREEPOST CN81, Croydon, CR9 3WZ

Offer valid in UK only and is not available to current Mills & Boon® Reader Service™subscribers to this series. Overseas and Eire please write for details. We reserve the right to refuse an application and applicants must be aged 18 years or over. Only one application per household. Terms and prices subject to change without notice. Offer expires 31st January 2008. As a result of this application, you may receive offers from Harlequin Mills & Boon and other carefully selected companies. If you would prefer not to share in this opportunity please write to The Data Manager at PO Box 676, Richmond, TW9 1WU.

Mills & Boon® is a registered trademark owned by Harlequin Mills & Boon Limited.
Blaze® is being used as a registered trademark owned by Harlequin Mills & Boon Limited.
The Mills & Boon® Reader Service™ is being used as a trademark.